BLOOD CODE

A Thrilling Novel By

RICK SIMONDS

D1384496

ISBN-10 0-615-44178-5
ISBN-13 9780615441788

ACKNOWLEDGEMENTS

Writing a novel has long been a dream of mine. Like many who have read thousands of murder-mysteries, I was sure that this was to be my genre of choice. While all characters and events in this book are fictitious and any similarities to real persons, living or dead, is coincidental and not intended by the author, as with all writers, they are drawn from a lifetime of observation.

I quickly found out that *writing* a book can be a daunting task especially when it deals with expertise and protocol outside the boundaries of one's knowledge. For that reason on several occasions I turned to good friend Joe Loughlin, a former lead detective for the Portland Police Department and co-author of *Finding Amy*. He not only answered many of my questions but also put me in touch with Matt Stewart, formerly a detective with the Maine State Police who provided much-needed information.

Another friend, Bruce Coffin, a Portland Police Officer who couldn't go away on vacation without being pestered, was also involved. Bruce offered many suggestions and advice all of which proved helpful. He and his wife Karen were among the first to read the work in progress and provided much encouragement. An accomplished artist, he also provided the design for the cover of this book. His outstanding work can be viewed at www.coffincreations.com.

Another individual who deserves to be mentioned is the commanding officer of the Maine State Police's Troop B, Lt. Walter Grzyb, who provided many answers via telephone and was more than willing to share his knowledge.

One final police detective who read, encouraged and offered suggestions is Steve Webster, a supervisor of the Criminal Investigation Division for the South Portland Police Department. He is also the President of Maine Association of Police and author of *One Promise Kept,* an exciting account of some of his most memorable cases.

Lastly, and most significantly, because she was forced to listen to my constant queries about changes in plot, dialogue possibilities, and story line considerations, while taking away from together-time, I want to acknowledge the contributions of my wife, Sherry. She provided suggestions, support and solace in equal doses which kept me going through the time it took to write this book.

The following books were used in research for this novel:
The Code Book by Simon Singh. Doubleday, 1999
The Encyclopedia of Serial Killers by Michael Newton. Chekmark Books, 2000
The Encyclopedia of Serial Killers by Brian Lane and Wilfred Gregg. Berkley Books 1992

DEDICATION

One of the neat things about writing a book is that one gets an opportunity to dedicate the writing of it to whomever he or she wants. In this case I would like to dedicate Blood Code to my parents, Dwight and Winifred Simonds.

My Mom is the reason that I love the written word because she read to me incessantly when I was young. She remains, at 89 years old, a passionate reader with an active mind.

My Dad, Si, who died in 2000, was my inspiration, my friend and my guiding light. Every day was a blessing to him and he shared that zest with all whom he came in contact. Few days go by without my thinking of him.

ABOUT THE AUTHOR

Rick Simonds is known on many fronts. While *Blood Code* is his first novel, he has been an accomplished writer for many years with stints as a columnist for both The Maine Sunday Telegram and Horseman and Fair World and on many occasions as a feature writer for Hoof Beats Magazine. He has written three children's books as well as a collection of poems and personal memoirs.

He graduated from the University of Southern Maine where he earned both a B.S. in English and M.S. in Educational Administration.

For 24 years he served as a college basketball coach at both Saint Joseph's College in Maine and Davidson College in North Carolina. He retired from that in 2003 with an overall winning percentage of .726 which is sixth all-time in NCAA Division III. He also coached high school basketball at both Ellsworth and Bonny Eagle. He served as assistant coach for the Portland Mountain Cats and as both Head Coach and General Manager of the Portland Wave, both of which were in the professional ranks of the USBL. On 17 occasions he won Coach of the Year Honors.

He has been inducted into the University of Southern Maine Athletic Hall of Fame as a player and both the Saint Joseph's College Hall of Fame and New England Basketball Hall of Fame as a coach.

He currently resides in Southern Maine with his wife, Sherry and son Steven. Also a part of his family are daughters Lisa and Sarah, step-daughters Macie and Holly and a special grandson, Zachary. Pets Sammi and Evan have begged to be included.

In addition to being an English and Creative Writing teacher at the high school level and selling real estate for Pleasant River Properties in Windham he also serves as the color commentator for the NBA D league, Maine Red Claws on WJAB radio and Time Warner television broadcasts.

~ PROLOGUE ~

The light rain falling from the sky camouflaged the tears that ran from Reed Sanderson's eyes. Although the temperature was seasonably warm his broad shoulders were hunched to shield the shudders that wracked his body. Burying a young child will bring even the strongest and bravest to tears.

Reed's right arm was draped over the shoulder of his son, Scott, while his wife Amy was on his left arm clinging to his dark rain coat. Her sun glasses belied the weather but did little to mask the pain that coursed through her body. In front of the small assemblage was a closed casket prepared to be lowered into the silent, waiting orifice.

Nearby, Jake Lewis stood, his hands folded reverently in front of him, his right hand on top, squeezing the fingers of his left. He, too, felt overcome with the loss of someone very close but his body ached also with agonizing feelings of guilt. *This just can't be,* he thought. *There was no reason for Tommy Sanderson to die.*

The minister overseeing the ceremony continued to speak but Reed heard little of what was being said. It was certainly not his first funeral but there is nothing that prepares one for the death of a young child, *your child.* He wanted to be strong for those around him and although he thought he was all cried-out from the church service, he clung to those on both sides and did not attempt to hide the tears that flowed freely.

When he was finished the minister walked over to the family and softly offered words of condolence. Reed nodded politely, more concerned with Scott who was now crying uncontrollably. He wrapped him in his arms and pulled him close. Amy, too, wrapped her arms around the young boy and together the three of them stood as one, clinging and sobbing as the attendants lowered the wooden box into the ground.

Jake, like Reed a detective in the Maine State Police, was one of the few in attendance who were not family members and, as the Sandersons slowly began to wend their way toward their car, he walked toward them. He tenderly wrapped his massive arms around Amy and then Scott before stepping toward Reed. He threw his arms around his best friend and the two embraced in a primal squeeze as if they might be able to wring the pain from their respective souls. After several seconds Jake leaned back, looked into Reed's eyes and whispered, " I'll get the bastard who did this."

~ 1 ~

Death is usually such a private passage, he thought. *Silent and Somber. It is such a pleasure to be able to share in the planning, the preparation... the ceremony.*

The "painter" pulled his chair up closer to his "canvas," which was actually the white-painted wall in the living room of a small studio apartment.. He painted with patience and precision, his eye for detail clearly demonstrated. He wanted this to be *just right.*

The broad strokes of his brush danced across the latex surface bringing a smile to his face. The crimson streaks, a series of steady-handed lines and figures, turned blackish as they met the air and were oxygenated. His brush was a small plastic-bristled model that he had brought with him for the occasion.

Below him on the hard wood floor lie sprawled a dark-complexioned young lady who most would have considered attractive had it not been for the gaping wound on her neck stretching from ear to ear and leaking the dark liquid the killer was using for "paint."

Both of her carotid arteries had been severed when he walked up behind her, held her head in a vice-like grip with his left arm, and raked the serrated edge of a carving knife under her chin in one brisk motion. He had released her after her body was finished spasming and laid her on the floor. He unbuttoned her blouse, put his knife under the center of her bra and pulled, snapping it in half. He pulled it off of her body and brought it up next to his face inhaling the girl's aroma, a mixture of perfume and perspiration.

He glanced down at the dead girl, blood congealing around her body, and smiled. He then bent to make one last circular incision around her nipple, effectively removing one breast. Pleased with himself and the artwork on the wall he lifted the brush and made one final stroke to dot the letter "I" and walked out of the apartment being sure to shut off the light and close the door carefully behind him. The venerable wedding song, "We've only just begun" ran through his mind.

~ 2 ~

"Hey, Dad. When we get there can we go fishing right away?"

Reed Sanderson looked in the rearview mirror, made eye contact with his fourteen year old son and smiled. "We will, Scott. I promise. Are you afraid there won't be any fish left."

The boy matched his dad's smile with one of his own, his blue eyes glistening.

"If there aren't, it won't be because your dad has caught them," offered the boy's grandfather with a prolonged chuckle from the front seat. "He couldn't catch a fish in the bathtub."

"Sandy, it isn't quite that bad and why is it that you get such a kick out of your own jokes?"

The seventy-five year old man, whose real name was David, but who *everyone* called Sandy, adjusted his glasses and rubbed his hand across his head to rearrange the few white hairs that had refused to succumb to age. Crows feet grew from the corner of his eyes, a tribute to his ready smile.

"Most people just don't have as advanced a sense of humor as I do. I'm one of the few who get my jokes," he offered with a widening grin.

Reed rolled his eyes in the way of good-natured fun and thought what a wonderful opportunity he was about to enjoy. Three generations of Sandersons heading off to the Maine woods for fun, fishing and fellowship. The truth was that Reed didn't enjoy fishing as much as he enjoyed spending time with his father and son, but with his job as Sergeant in the Criminal Investigation Division of the Maine State Police these times were few and far between.

Reed had purchased a small cottage on the shore of Moose Lake after he returned from the service nearly twenty years ago. Not sure what he wanted to do with his psychology degree from Dartmouth, he had entered the Navy and become part of the Naval Criminal Investigative Service. He served as a psychoanalyst, a practitioner who made connections in a patient's unconscious or subconscious mind and helped solve several cases. He enjoyed the work and when his time was up the decision to join the State Police afterward seemed an easy one.

In the beginning he and his wife, Amy, had snuck away to the cottage for romantic "furloughs," as he liked to call them, but then came the boys and an increasingly busy schedule and those interludes became rare. Since Amy had left him some months ago he had not been back.

This was all about to change, he thought, as he rolled down the window in his 2007 Ford Explorer and let the wind blow his thick, prematurely-white hair. "Stately" is what ladies generally called it but with his piercing blue eyes and chiseled jaw Sandy liked to joke that Reed looked like Leslie Nielsen of *Naked Gun* fame. Thanks to being a former high school football player, and to his stint in the Navy, Reed possessed an athletic build with wide shoulders and narrow waist that he maintained through a regimen of consistent weight training and occasional jogging.

Because he enjoyed wearing plaid or window pane shirts with his jeans, Amy liked to say that he was Ted Danson's older brother and that he should be working at *Cheers*. At six feet two and a solid one hundred and ninety pounds he recognized that he did resemble Danson in several ways but when he playfully responded to Amy, he acknowledged that not everyone knew *his* name.

Marvin Gaye's *Sexual Healing* came on the radio and Reed cranked it up to a near-deafening volume. He knew that with a fourteen year old listening there might be those who would disapprove but he had always treated his sons as young men, and besides, it was a great song.

The Explorer was packed full with camping equipment, clothing, and enough food, according to Sandy, to "feed an army." In the backseat beside Scott, lie Barney a six-month old black lab who had been given to them after the "accident" by Jake.

"Every boy needs a dog, Reed," he explained, "and besides, it'll serve as a buddy for Scott."

He was right, of course, and although it couldn't fill the void, it was a good companion.

And, as Sandy observed, "he'll help teach Scott life's lessons."

"Hey Dad, can Barney and I get out here and walk to the camp.

Barney's been cooped up and needs to stretch."

"Sure, Scott. He could probably use the exercise. Hop out. We'll meet you down at the camp."

Barney bounded out of the SUV and headed straight for the longish grass beside the gravel way. Soon, he and Scott were racing down the road in an attempt to catch up to the Explorer. The tree-lined road ran for several hundred yards down to the cottage which sat but a few feet from the lake. Maine laws today prohibit such proximity but this knotty pine camp complete with three small bedrooms, living room, kitchen and porch was 'grandfathered' due to town ordinance.

"Ya' know, Sandy I'm worried about Scott. We've all been through a lot but it's been toughest on him. I know I've been looking forward to this for a long time so hopefully being here with the two of us will do him a world of good."

"I think it will do all of us some good, Reed, but Scott's a lot stronger than you're giving him credit for. He's going to be all right."

"I sure hope so, Dad. Say, why don't you get the boat ready while I unload the Explorer and put the gear away. We can get a couple of hours of fishing in before supper if we hustle."

Scott and Barney arrived at the camp just as Sandy was backing the trailer into the water and unhooking the 24 foot Sport Craft 242 from the SUV. As the boat floated free from the trailer Sandy took a line from the bow and pulled the boat toward the wooden dock which ran out into the water. It was not a new boat but was perfect for their needs as it had a cuddy cabin, ideal if the weather turned, along with an enclosed head and room to move around on. The 260 horsepower Mercury provided plenty of power if necessary and at times Reed felt it was more boat than they needed but this was not one of them.

"I'll take it, Sandy, shouted Scott as he jogged down the planks, Barney close behind.

"Sounds good to me, Scotty. Tie 'er up. Your dad will be here soon with the fishing poles and gas." The old man climbed back into the driver's seat of the Explorer and pulled the metal trailer out of the water.

Reed came out of the camp wearing a khaki vest and a like-colored fishing hat with a variety of fishing lures and flies distributed around the brim. He had three fishing poles and a small Coleman cooler in one hand, a tackle box and gas can in the other and under one arm was a small net.

"Did L.L. Bean have a sale or is there a photo shoot scheduled for this afternoon?" asked Sandy with his tongue planted firmly in his cheek.

"You need to dress the part if you're going to catch the big fish," Reed replied. "All I'm missing," he continued, "is a tape measure and a scale to measure my record breakers."

"You know, Reed," Sandy retorted, "if you're looking to break records you might want a stack of 45's and a hammer."

Scott's high-pitched laughter echoed across the lake as the three boarded the boat and pushed off the dock. They had forgotten all about Barney until they saw him swimming after the boat, paws churning, with just his head above the water. When he got alongside Reed reached down, picked him up and placed him in the boat. Barney repaid the favor by shaking off all over them eliciting howls and more laughter.

Fall comes early to Western Maine and the harvest-colored leaves surrounding the lake formed a perfect frame for the refulgent diamond reflections of the sun ricocheting off the rippling waters. Several other small boats buoyed merrily on the lake, fisherman clinging to a last vestige of warm weather and calm waters.

They had been slowly trolling close to shore in communal silence when Scott quietly asked, "Dad, will you and Mom get back together?"

"Whoa, where did that come from, buddy?"

"It's just hard, Dad. I love living with you and Sandy but I love Mom too, and it bothers me that she is all alone."

"It bothers me too, Scott, and you know that her being away is not what I want. But ever since Tommy died she has blamed me for his death and has decided that as long as I am still with the State Police she wants no part of us being together. My whole life has been in law enforcement and I'm not ready to retire."

"Do you still love her, Dad?"

"Today, more than yesterday. I know it's been hard on her but it's been hard on all of us and I don't feel that walking out on us is the way to handle it. My Mom and Dad taught me that if you have a problem then you sit down and talk it out. Isn't that right, Sandy?"

"Communication, Scotty, is the key to relationships," the old man replied. "Never go to bed mad, never leave without saying 'I love you.' I've always espoused that formula, both with your grandmother, when she was alive, and with your father."

"Hey, look at this fishing rod!" interrupted Reed as his line bowed and the tip of the pole dove into the edge of the water.

"Finally, Dad, maybe you have something."

"Oh, I've got something all right. It feels like a tuna."

"To make that comparison, one would have actually had to catch a tuna," proposed Sandy.

"You know what I mean," countered Reed. "You may want to grab your camera Scott, *Field and Stream* will want visual proof of this beauty."

"Why aren't you playing it, Dad? Reel it in."

"I'm trying to, it's just too heav.... here it comes."

There was a release of tension on the line and Reed worked feverishly to reel in this "beauty." Seconds later a used tire broke the surface, Reed's hook solidly fastened into the edge of the rubber sphere.

Scott's face broke into a wide grin but before he could say anything Sandy chimed in,

"Don't put that camera away, Scotty, ole boy. *Field and Stream* may not be interested but I'll bet *Car & Driver* will want that photo."

~ 3 ~

The morning sun chased away the darkness leaving a trail of pink and purple streaks. The crisp, clear air lent credence to the State's slogan; 'Maine - The Way Life Should Be.'

Reed was up early throwing kindling into the wood stove to take the chill off the camp. Sandy, too, had risen early and dressed in worn jeans and red plaid shirt, was frying bacon on the stove in one pan while several small trout were browning in another.

"Looks like another beautiful day, Reed. What time do you want to hit the lake?" Reed reached for the coffee maker and poured himself a cup. "Let's let Scott sleep in a bit, Sandy. I'll take Barney out while you finish cooking breakfast."

"Sounds good. I think I'll make up a few sandwiches to take with us."

It was almost three hours later that Reed gently shook his son in an effort to wake him. Reed had long marveled at a growing teenager's ability to sleep through the sights, sounds and smells of family activities.

"Wake up, Scott."

"Wh ...what time is it?"

"Time to get up - it's almost noon. The fish have made several calls to see if we're coming out."

"Yea, added Sandy. For them it's like a Bob Marley show - a comedic performance with a Maine theme." Scott threw on some clothes and was half-heartedly brushing his teeth when Reed's cell phone rang. He reached into his pocket, removed the phone and glanced at the number that registered. "Oh, Damn!" he muttered.

"Who is it Reed?" asked Sandy.

"It's the office. I've got to take it. I told them not to call unless it was important..."

"What's up, Callie?"

"Sorry to ruin your day, Reed, but you better get back here. I'm afraid we've got a problem."

Reed listened as Callie Canizzaro, the dispatcher, or ECS - Emergency Communication Specialist - for Reed's unit relayed the unpleasant message. The state was divided into three divisions and since Reed worked out of the Southern Division he was one of the two primary investigators for all homicides in that region with the exception of those committed in Portland, Maine's largest city.

"A young woman's body was found a few minutes ago. She was cut real bad, Reed, and that's not all - there's a note."

"Oh Callie, this couldn't possibly have come at a worse time, but I'll be there. Where am I going?"

As Callie relayed the address in Gorham, Reed saw the disappointment register on his son's face. He hung up the phone. "Scott, I'm so sorry but there's been a murder and I have to go back. I'll make it up to you, honest I will."

"Dad, I know that it's not your fault but do you have to go to this one? Can't you say no – just this once?"

Reed looked away, out at the lake, before answering wistfully, "I wish that I could Scott, I wish I could."

~ 4 ~

"What kind of a sick bastard would do this?" Steve Mangino, a forensic expert and part of the Evidence Response Team, voiced the words that were being thought by many as the crime unit went about their business taking photographs, dusting for prints and looking for other minutia of evidence that may have been left behind.

"I can't imagine," answered Reed to the seemingly rhetorical question, as he entered the crime scene. "What do we know about the victim?"

Jake Lewis, a grizzly bear disguised as a man, with short-cropped dark hair that stood up spiked in front and thick dark eyebrows that ran straight across his forehead like a wooly caterpillar, walked into the room. A twenty year veteran of the force, he attempted to provide some answers. "She's been identified as Angela Carrington, twenty-three years old, a junior at the University of Southern Maine. She lived here with a roommate, Nicole Wood, who hasn't been located. We're tracking down her parents through the University."

"Who found the body?"

"The girl's mother. It was her birthday on Friday and when the girl didn't respond to repeated calls she drove over. The ME says that there is no greenish tint to the skin so, based on the lividity, he estimates the time of death to be 30-36 hours ago making it between 10:00 pm Thursday and 4:00 am Friday."

"What else do we have?"

"It looks like the animal that did this was inside the place waiting for her or else she knew her attacker and let him in. There's no sign of forced entry or sign of a struggle. He must have come up behind her and slit her throat. Both arteries were severed and she bled out. By the looks of the wounds it's something ragged, possibly a knife with a serrated edge. He may have used one of the knives from a butcher block set on her counter, there's one missing. The entire set has been taken to the lab to be examined."

"Anybody in the other apartments see anything, Jake?"

"We've got uniforms interviewing everyone in the building as well as the others in the neighborhood but no word yet. Say, I'm surprised to see you here so soon. Had you arrived at the camp?"

"We got there yesterday. We were just getting ready to go back out on the lake"

"You've been planning that for awhile. How's Scotty doing?"

"Just okay. He understands but is pretty disappointed that we had to leave. I think I feel worse than he does. I need to spend some quality time with him after what happened. I just can't seem to catch a break, uh, - Callie said there was a note."

"Actually it's a painted message on the back of this wall. Based on the blood trail it appears that he killed her in the living room and dragged her over here. The two walked around the short half-wall that separated the kitchen from the living room and stared at the carefully painted message on the smooth surface.

Behold the death o' heathens
think of when indelible liabilities wilt
loving can begin whither preparations
shroud before deserving just fruit divine

"Whatta ya' make of this, Reed? It looks like he used her blood to 'paint' the message."

"Can you imagine having the balls to sit and paint a message after having killed a human being?"

A photographer was taking pictures of the wall as the two men examined it. A man behind him was video taping the same scene.

"Just what we need - a murderer who wants to play games. Hopefully it's a one-time thing. But, ya' know Jake, I somehow doubt it."

A uniformed officer walked into the room and handed Reed a note. "We were able to get in touch with Nicole Wood's parents and then Nicole. She was in Boston visiting her boy friend this weekend and said she left Thursday after work. She's on her way back. Here's her cell phone number along with that of her parents."

Reed took the piece of paper from the officer, folded it and put it in his front pocket. If there is anything a police officer detests, Reed thought, it is having to make a phone call notifying friends or family of the death of a loved one.

~ 5 ~

Reed drove with a feeling of dread and déjà vu in the pit of his stomach. He felt like stopping for a beer but thought better of it and headed for home. He had put in a long day and it was almost midnight as he pulled into the driveway of his three bedroom ranch in Raymond. He intended to sneak into the house so as not to not disturb its inhabitants but he needn't have worried as Sandy met him at the front door.

"Sandy, what are you doing up?"

"I thought you might like some company," Sandy offered. "I'm sure today was tough for you all around."

"Thanks, Dad," said Reed, as he sat on the sofa in the living room and started to untie his shoes.

Sandy returned from the kitchen with two Newcastle Brown Ales and sat in a solid oak mission antique rocker facing his son. Reed took a long pull from the amber bottle, wiped his mouth with the back of his hand and asked, "How's Scott doing?"

"He's alright. We played a couple of games of cribbage and watched some T.V. After dinner he text-messaged some of his friends and went to bed early. He was pretty upset but he understands. He'll be okay."

"I hope so, Dad. I just don't know. Ever since Tommy died and his mother left …" his voice trailed off. "I don't know what I would do without you, Dad."

Sandy rose from his chair, put one arm around Reed's neck, and gave a little tug.

"You'd do just fine just like before I moved in, and besides, my guess is that Amy will come to her senses soon and there'll be no need for an old coot like me."

"I hope you're right Sandy, about Amy I mean, but ever since Tommy was killed things just haven't been the same with her. She blames me."

"It takes time, Reed. Tommy was her first born. She'll be back but you need to be understanding and patient. And Reed, …"

"Yea"

"The fish are appreciative of your being busy."

~ 6 ~

On average there are 20-25 homicides committed in Maine in any given year, 90% of which are solved by the 39 detectives in the CID. The first two days they had set up a command post in the offices of the Gorham Police Department but now they had moved to their "home" and sitting around a long conference table in the Southern Division headquarters in Gray were seven of the detectives assigned to that unit.

Each Division has a Lieutenant and two Sergeants divided by counties and Reed was in charge of Cumberland and York Counties. He stood in front of the group, a red-patterned tie offering contrast to his blue oxford shirt and light gray trousers. Above him, on a white wall, was the message left by Angela Carrington's killer cast by an overhead projector.

"Anybody have any thoughts on our note," began Reed.

"Were there any prints?" asked Tom Lombardo, a heavy set detective with round, ruddy face and a handle bar mustache in which he took great pride.

"None," replied Reed, putting down his cup of coffee. "In fact, there were none at the crime scene. It seems our killer must have worn gloves which certainly points to it being pre- meditated. The autopsy indicates that it was probably done by one of the knives from the butcher block set on the victim's counter but the missing knife hasn't been located."

"What did we find out about Nicole Wood, the roommate," asked Jake who worked the crime scene with Reed. "And what about Angela - did she have any boy friends?"

"Nicole checked out," answered Reed. "She left right from her job at the Maine Mall Thursday to go to visit her boyfriend in Waltham, Mass. She said that the last time she saw Angela was that morning but they had talked by cell phone while she was driving south. Angela was home doing some homework and said nothing about anyone coming to visit. She had dated some, but not recently, and had no boyfriend," according to Nicole. We also interviewed the victim's parents but have no firm leads there, either. She's been living on her own for a while."

"As for the note," began Walt Wizkowski, or "Wiz" to his friends and fellow detectives, "I've studied it for a long time but can't seem to make heads nor tails of it."

While the Maine State Police has no resident experts in cryptology they all had taken courses on the subject and it was a particular item of interest for Wizkowski. He had recently returned from the FBI Academy in Quantico, Virginia where he had studied with the Cryptanalysis and Racketeering Records Unit (CRRU) which provides assistance to all levels of enforcement agencies. They read together:

Behold the death o' heathens
think of when indelible liabilities wilt
loving can begin whither preparations
shroud before deserving just fruit divine

Reed took a laser pointer and turned it on focusing a red dot under 'Behold.' "Let's take it line by line," he suggested. "If you have any ideas bounce 'em off me."

"It seems to me," Wiz began, "that there are key words in each line. 'death o' heathens' is an unusual turn of phrase. A heathen is 'an unconverted member of a people or nation that does not acknowledge God,' but does he refer to himself or the victim as the heathen?"

"That's good, Wiz. What else?" asked Reed.

"It seems that 'indelible liabilities' refers to the victim. Indelible means permanent or cannot be obliterated and certainly the death of Angela is permanent."

"And the killer must feel she was a liability," chimed in Jake.

"To whom? And 'wilt' - usually that refers to a flower," suggested Joe Quinn. Wizkowski again spoke. "'Loving can begin' seems biblical, as with the acceptance of God; possibly another point of reference to a heathen being converted. The word *whither* seems unusual. It was used in poetry in older times meaning to what point, place or result, but it has been replaced by the word 'where.'"

"I remember, now why I hated poetry, piped in Lombardo. '*To wit, whither thine loveth,*' just didn't cut it for me. I never did understand what they were trying to say," he laughed.

The group joined in the laughter but Reed brought them back to the task at hand.

"What *is* important is that we figure out what the sick bastard that wrote this is trying to say - before it's too late."

"You think there will be others?" asked Frank Durgin, the newest addition to the division.

"I have no doubt," responded Reed. "This message is a challenge to us, alright. He is taunting us and believes that he is smarter than we are. Based on the damage done to the genitalia of the victim, done post mortem according to the autopsy, he is an angry man. He didn't want to just kill Angela he wanted to desecrate her. By dragging her into the kitchen where she would be seen upon entrance, he was further putting her on display. We all know that using a knife to kill someone means it's personal. If that wasn't enough he went ahead and cut off a breast. There is a lot going on in his demented mind. Wiz, whatta ya' have for the last line?"

"Well, 'shroud' relates to dressing for a burial service and the expression 'just fruit' usually is interchanged with 'just rewards' and implies that someone had something coming to them."

"Do you suppose that this refers to the death of Angela being a sacrifice in order to put himself in an even better position?" asked Jake. "Or could it be that he feels he is acting God-like by killing her?"

"I suppose that it could be either, but what that position is, or his rationale is, I have no idea. What I do know," said Reed, placing the laser pointer on the conference table, "is that we had better figure it out ... and soon."

~ 7 ~

It had been a productive, if not eventful, day thought Reed as he climbed into the Explorer.

If only real crimes could be solved like they are on television. I wait days, or even weeks, for reports to come back from the lab and good ole' Horatio on CSI Miami only needs to wait ten or fifteen minutes. No wonder he gets paid so much money. Hell, even Columbo, with his wrinkled trench coat and bumbling interrogations, used to wrap them up in an hour. I really need to work on my skills.

As he pulled into his driveway his cell phone rang and as he put the receiver to his ear a sense of warmth coursed through him. It was Amy, his high school sweetheart and wife

"Hi Reed," she began.

"Hey, Amy. What's up?"

"I just heard about the horrible murder of that USM student. I wanted to call to see if you are alright."

"Well, my knee has been bothering me a little bit."

"Reed, You know what I mean."

"Amy, Listen. If you're asking me if I'm able to do my job, the answer is yes. If you're asking, does it tear me up because it reminds me of Tommy, the answer is yes. If you're asking me if I'm doing alright without you the answer is NO! He didn't know why he hung up the phone on her because it wasn't like him. He was sorry the second that he had done it. But not so sorry that he dialed the number back. He lied awake well into the night before finally succumbing to sleep's embrace.

~ 8 ~

Susan Weeks met Reed as he walked in the door of the unit. The competent, though officious, troop secretary served in a variety of roles and was convinced that she was the reason the unit was able to function. She served as an office manager and often volunteered to do anything that needed to be done in order to ingratiate herself into the doings of those she worked with.

Dressed in a short khaki skirt and flowered blouse she was either mildly, or highly, attractive depending on whether the judge was a stranger or herself looking in a mirror. She was in her mid-forties, considered herself much younger and dressed accordingly, often forgetting to button the top button or three on her blouses. She wore her strawberry blonde hair so short and received so many raised eyebrows the first time she wore it to work that the guys were convinced that she was making a political statement.

As the mother of a teenaged daughter who had been divorced for several years, she liked to be thought of as "one of the guys" yet personally wanted to attract *one of the guys* which often led to consternation around the office. Reed had noticed a slight behavioral change in Susan since Amy had left him but hadn't found a reason to speak to her - yet.

"Reed, Charlie Carrington, Angela's father, is here and he is upset," she said. "He wants to know what you're doing to find his daughter's killer."

"Where is he, Susan?"

"I gave him a cup of coffee and told him to wait in the conference room. He's been here about ten minutes."

Reed looked through the one-way rectangular window into the conference room and saw a short, but fit, man in his mid to late forties pacing back and forth. He had a narrow face, graying crew-cut and a "Jamaican Me Crazy" tan. He wore amber-tinted glasses pushed up onto his hair, a blue oxford shirt with crested navy "CWC" in a monogram on his pocket, charcoal gray cotton trousers and oxford tassel loafers. His lemon cashmere sweater rested across the back of his shoulders with the two arms draped and lightly tied in front just below a gold medallion hanging off a gold chain.

Reed opened the door to the conference room and entered. "Hello, Mr. Carrington, Reed Sanderson. What can I do for you?"

"What can you do? Why, you can catch the sonofabitch who murdered my daughter. That's what you can do."

"I assure you, Mr. Carrington, that we are doing everything we can to find whoever is responsible," Reed responded, in a voice purposely calm in an attempt to assuage the distraught man in front of him.

"Well, It's obviously not enough. I work in Maine and there is no excuse for this - no need for this. 'The Way Life Should Be,' my ass. My baby suffered and I want to see the bastard fry that did this to her. You know," he continued, waggling one finger at Reed. "I am one of the Governor's biggest contributors and he has assured me that he would spare no expense." With that, he stormed out of the conference room and as he prepared to leave the building he turned and took one last parting shot. "You don't know what it's like to lose a child, Sergeant, because if you did you'd have caught him by now."

Reed glared at the man exiting the building but said nothing. Susan came over and gave him a hug as the three troopers in the room watched incredulously as the door slammed.

~ 9 ~

Carrie Mortenson picked up her pace as she jogged along the forest trail surrounding the campus of Bowdoin College. *This school had been a good choice*, she thought, as she bounded along. It was tough to get into, but her first year had been marked by good grades and she had made many new friends. She felt invigorated as she pumped her arms and legs, a soft breeze blowing her short blonde hair and cooling her face.

Three hundred more yards 'til the end of the trail and then I'll sprint across the athletic fields to the dorm, she thought.

The warm, late afternoon sun filtered through the tall pines, for which Bowdoin was known, the needles beneath her feet forming a rust-colored carpet. She breathed deeply the pine scent, a sense of accomplishment engulfing her.

Two hundred yards to go. I see a hot shower in my future.

She never saw the man step out from behind the giant pine and throw a cross-body block into her legs. She extended her arms as she tried to maintain her balance but was unable to succeed. Gasping for breath she tried to scream but he was on her before she could fill her lungs with air. Together they rolled across the path. He climbed onto her stomach, his weight holding her down as she struggled for freedom. She reached wildly, her arms flailing until her right hand contacted skin, her fingernails raking his cheek and drawing blood. "Ow, you stupid bitch!" he screeched in surprise and anger.

He swung violently at her landing a solid punch on her right cheek, the bone crunching like a bag of potato chips. With blood and spittle dripping from the side of her mouth and a deep gurgle resonating from her throat she was clinging to the last vestige of life as he withdrew his knife from it's sheath. The last image her eyes reflected, before she lapsed into death's darkness, was that of a serrated carving knife being plunged into her chest.

The killer dragged her limp body off the trail into the under brush, removed her clothing, and took care of some unfinished business. He then propped her body up against a pine tree like a straw figure that people in Maine place against bales of hay for Halloween.

He found a pine bough and swept the pathway eliminating any signs of a struggle and then checked to make sure there were no distinguishable footprints from his worn-smooth footwear. Next, he pulled his blood-stained overalls down his body and threw them, along with her clothes, into a gym bag he had placed behind the tree. He then removed a previously designed note from his pants pocket. He carefully held it against her lower abdomen and then pushed the knife once again to hold the note in place like a pet owner might fasten a "Missing Dog" sign on a telephone pole. He removed his plastic gloves and threw those into the bag.

Satisfied, he back-tracked to his vehicle.

~ 10 ~

The town of Brunswick is a bucolic burgh of 25,000 inhabitants on the Androscoggin River. While it boasts having the widest Main Street in America it is actually better known for being the home of Joshua Chamberlain and Bowdoin College, the former a Civil War General who made his name defending Little Round Top at the Battle of Gettysburg, and the latter one of the more selective private liberal arts institutions in the country.

The Brunswick Police Department, when fully staffed, has 35 officers, seven of whom are detectives. Since two of them are school resource officers and one other is a juvenile detective it is easy to understand why the department, in many people's eyes, has long felt a personnel crunch impacting its ability to provide satisfactory service to the community.

Reed was just finishing getting dressed when he received a call from Tim Stockwell, one of Brunswick's detectives and a friend of Reed's going back over twenty years. Although he was quite a bit older than Reed they had on several occasions worked together on cases.

"Hey, Reed. I'm afraid we have a problem down here. A Bowdoin student was found murdered this morning. I don't know any more yet but I'm going over there now. You may want to head down."

"Thanks, Tim. Will do. I'll see you in a few minutes." Reed jumped in his car and headed northeast while dialing Jake on his cell phone.

"Mornin' Jake. Have you heard about the homicide in Brunswick?"

"Sure have, in fact, I just got here. It's as you feared, Reed. It appears we have a serial killer on our hands. You better get here quick."

"I'm on my way. Who found her?"

"A couple of students out for a jog, I'm told. They notified

Campus Security who got in touch with us. It seems that she was pretty well known and has been identified as Carrie Mortenson from Reading, Massachusetts."

"Who's on the scene?"

"The Brunswick police have it cordoned off until our people get here."

"How long ago was she killed?"

"Too early to tell. Security tells us that she has been missing since yesterday afternoon. They have the names and addresses of her roommate and friends compiled for us."

"You said it was by the same killer, Jake. What makes you think so?"

"There was another note – with the same type of cryptic clues."

"Christ Oh Mighty! The press will be all over this. Just what we need is some wacko killing college girls. Did he use a knife?"

"Yea, Reed but this time he left it at the scene."

"Oh?"

"He used the goddamn knife to hold the note, Reed. He stuck it right in her stomach. And Reed – there's one other thing."

"What's that?"

"He cut off her right hand at the wrist – and he took it with him!"

~ 11 ~

When Reed arrived at the crime scene it looked like all hell had broken loose. There were campus security officers, Brunswick town police, most of the detectives from his unit, and reporters and photographers from three of the four networks that served Maine, all engaged in performing their duties. *All that was needed,* he thought, *was a high-wire act and a dancing bear to make the circus complete.*

A circle of yellow police tape delineated the crime scene in which there were five evidence technicians wearing plastic suits and gloves; one leaning over the body of the young girl, two others on their hands and knees looking for shards of evidence. In addition there was one taking photos and one videotaping the entire scene.

Sawhorses had been set up on both ends of the campus trail some 50 yards from the proximity of the crime scene, behind which stood citizens of the community, students and college employees. A photographer employed by the MSP as part of the Evidence Response Team was taking shots in all directions hoping to capture the perpetrator on film posing as one of the incident bystanders. It had been proven on many occasions that the person responsible wished to see what the police were doing to capture him.

Lisa Landsburg, an attractive and well-known anchor from Eyewitness News, recognized Reed and thrust her microphone into his face. "Sgt. Sanderson," she began, "this is the second Maine college student this week to meet foul play. Are the cases related?"

Caught off guard Reed smiled and replied, "It's much too early to determine that, Lisa. We have not even completed our preliminary investigation here as you can see. I'm sure that we will have some information for you later in the day." Other reporters, seeing that he was "on air," began to migrate toward him but before they could get close enough he turned his back to the camera and said quietly, "Don't ever put me on the spot like that. If you want to interview me, you ask first."

As Reed turned and walked away he saw Jake speaking to a Campus Security officer.

"Hey, Reed. Meet Walker Gray the head of Security here on campus."

"Nice to meet you, Walker. Sorry it's under such difficult circumstances. Do you have any more information on the young lady who was killed?"

"The victim is Carrie Mortenson, a sophomore from Reading, Massachusetts and the daughter of Ben and Sarah Mortenson. She lives in 12 Stowe Hall and her roommate is Hannah Parisi. She may know now, since news travels fast on a college campus, but we purposely haven't been to see her. We thought we should leave that to you and your people."

"Thanks," he said. "We'll head over there now."

After getting directions to Stowe Hall, Reed and Jake headed the short distance away on foot.

"What do you think," asked Jake.

"I think we have a real sicko on our hands. I just hope he doesn't intend to make the rounds of all the colleges in Maine. That's all we need, mass hysteria."

~ 12 ~

Hannah Parisi was unaware of Carrie Mortenson's death when Reed knocked on her door a short while later. Tall and thin with straight brown hair to her shoulders and dark brown eyes, she was dressed in blue fleece pajama pants, a Bowdoin sweatshirt and pink bunny rabbit slippers. When told of her roommate's death Hannah broke down in chest-throbbing wails.

"Whyy?… Howw?… Oh my God, Why?… Do her parents know? How did it happen?"

Reed did not go into the details relative to the note or the particulars of her gruesome murder. He handed the girl his clean handkerchief and responded in almost a whisper.

"We are in the process of notifying her parents now, Hannah. She was found beside a jogging path behind the Farley Field house. I know this must be hard for you but it is important. Are you up to answering a few questions?"

"I… I'll try"

"Hannah, when was the last time you saw Carrie?"

"Yesterday afternoon – she was getting ready to go for a run. We talked about going to a movie but didn't make any definite plans."

"Did you expect her to come right back?"

"She is… was,… Oh God!… a good runner. Sometimes she would be gone for an hour or more. When she didn't come back I just assumed that she met up with someone and made other plans."

"Wouldn't she come back to shower first?"

"Usually, but occasionally she would run with someone else and then go to their residence hall to shower. We all share clothes with each other."

"You didn't find it strange that she didn't come back to sleep?"

"Not really, we have a circle of friends that we hang out with and we sleep over each other's rooms all the time."

"Wouldn't she have called you?"

"Generally, but I knew she didn't have her cell phone. She would leave it here when she went running. She said it just got in the way because she didn't want to talk while she was running. It's right there on the kitchen table … Oh Care…"

Again the girl began to cry and Reed paused for a minute to let her compose herself.

"I'm sorry Hannah … but just a few more … okay?"

"Uh huh"

"Did she have a boyfriend or was she seeing anyone on a regular basis?"

"Not really. She's done some dating and has an occasional hook-up but nothing serious."

"A hook-up?"

"Yea, you know. She'd meet up with some guy at a game or in the Union and then they'd come back here for the night or stay at his place. She had been seeing Sam Magee for awhile but they stopped seeing each other about three weeks ago. She said it was no big deal."

After writing that name in his notebook Reed asked, "Is there anyone that Carrie didn't get along with or that she may have had an argument with recently?"

"No one that I can think of …no, wait. She called campus security last week because she found a maintenance man in the girl's bathroom on our floor when she was showering. It was the second time he'd done it. We heard he got fired."

"Do you know his name?"

"No, but I'm sure that security can tell you."

"Hannah, you have been a great help but I'm afraid that we're going to have to go through her things with a fine tooth comb. We'll need to take her cell phone, computer and examine her things. Is there someone you can stay with while we complete our investigation? Is there any one you want us to call?"

"I'll be alright… as I said we have a circle of friends." As she thought about using the word *we* she again broke down in tears. "Who would want to hurt 'Care'… she was so nice to everyone. This is the second year we've been roommates and because we both live in Massachusetts we even do things together in the summer. We're like sisters."

After taking down the girl's cell phone number Reed paused

before leaving. "Thanks, Hannah. Here's my card. Let me know if there's anything I can do to help or if you think of anything else that might be important. If you decide to leave campus please, let us know where you can be reached. Oh, and Hannah, don't go anywhere alone."

~ 13 ~

The Painter rolled over on his mattress so that he could face the floor space heater on the other side of his room. He was used to sleeping with no pillow or blanket but he found some of the cold fall evenings took adjusting to.

He rose, urinated in the bucket provided and returned to the mattress, which also served as chair, table and anything else deemed necessary. He remembered how it had been difficult hitting the bucket with a hood on when he began long ago but now his instincts had been honed. On one occasion long ago he had removed the hood to go but he was caught doing that and for one week a spring clip was fastened to his testicles. He had passed out from the pain – and learned a lesson.

A while later he heard the tell-tale click of the basement door being opened and then footsteps descending the wooden steps. He was not sure if 'The Voice' would stop and speak but he sat still and silent. Soon a sonorous sound resonated into his room. He knew to listen very carefully and to pay strict attention to both directions and details. He knew better than to displease or disappoint 'The Voice' so he locked in on what he was being told.

After several minutes of instruction the lock on his door was undone and 'The Voice' disappeared. He removed his hood, stepped into his gray overall suit, pulled it up to his shoulders and fastened the buttons. Then, he put on his work boots, opened the door and turned to the right. He was, under no circumstances, to go left. Although he was curious to know what he would find if he had done so – he knew better.

He felt the adrenaline rush that came with a retreat from his lair. It wasn't the fresh air or the chance to drive the van – which he enjoyed a great deal – it was that he had been given the name of his next target.

He so looked forward to the visits and, more importantly, the messages he was given, because he knew they would lead to another adventure, another mission, another opportunity to earn the appreciation and gratitude he so desperately sought – he would not fail.

~ 14 ~

After going back to Campus Security Reed obtained a list of all the students living in Stowe Hall along with their pertinent information. He also was told that the name of the maintenance man found in Carrie's bathroom was Carmine Salvaggio. He and Jake stopped to read the report based on the girl's complaint which was dated five days ago.

The Human Resource office gave Salvaggio's address as 32 Meadowlark Lane in Harpswell which Reed soon found was a misnomer since he lived in a dilapidated trailer on a dirt road replete with pot-holes and rusted auto bodies on both sides.

It took Reed and Jake twenty minutes to find the location along Route 123 and as they traveled the last 100 yards along the dusty minefield they could see a lone light inside and a beat-up pick-up in front.

Salvaggio had indeed been let go by Bowdoin after serving three years in the custodial department. A background check showed that he had served in the army from which he left with a dishonorable discharge, had worked a battery of menial jobs over the years, and had recently gone through a divorce. According to the HR Department he was given two weeks severance pay following the recent complaint and a not-so-polite request not to return to campus.

It was reported that the forty-five year old had not taken kindly to his dismissal and insisted that he had done nothing wrong. According to his version on the report he had received a call telling him that the first floor bathroom was out of toilet paper and he had been replacing rolls in the stalls when "that girl" walked in to take a shower.

Reed shut off the car and the two detectives exited the cruiser quietly leaving their respective doors slightly ajar. Not knowing what type of reception he would receive, Reed walked cautiously toward the door, alert for any quick movements from within.

A thin, dusty Beagle was tied to the front of the trailer with a white clothes line and his baleful barking signaled their arrival. Jake held back staying close to the police-issued Impala as Reed went up the two wooden steps that served as an entryway, and knocked on the thin metal door.

There was no response to the knock although Reed could hear movement inside. He pointed for Jake to loop around toward the back of the trailer and knocked again – this time loudly enough to wake the dead on Bailey's Island.

"Who is it?" came the gruff reply from within.

"Reed Sanderson, Mr. Salvaggio… Maine State Police…. I'd like to ask you a few questions."

The door opened as far as the thin chain would allow and a grizzled face with stubble and pock marks leaned out. "I got nothin' to say. Leave me alone."

"Mr. Salvaggio … there's been a murder on the campus at Bowdoin and it was the girl that filed a complaint against you last week for being in her bathroom. Are you sure you don't want to speak to me for a minute?"

"I don't know nothin' 'bout no murder and I told ya,' I got nothin' to say." With that he slammed the door causing the entire trailer to shake.

Reed looked to his left and saw Jake standing at the end of the metallic gray trailer, his foot on the bumper of an old automobile semi-hidden in the long grass. Seconds later Salvaggio burst out of the back door on the opposite side of the trailer and began running through the field of dried grass. It took Jake but a matter of seconds to catch up to the small man and a flying tackle left him incapacitated. "It seems we have a runner," Jake said to Reed who had now caught up and was lifting Salvaggio to his feet.

"Now why do you suppose that is?"

"Is there a reason you're trying to get away, Mr. Salvaggio," asked Reed. "Is there something that you're not telling us?"

"Jake, put the cuffs on him and put him in the car while we make a protective sweep of his trailer. Certainly by him running we have a case of reasonable suspicion. We don't need a search warrant thanks to his actions and the plain view doctrine."

Jake fastened the cuffs, pushed his head down to get him in the back seat, and then joined Reed, who was waiting outside on the steps. They stepped inside and were immediately met with the stench of stale cigarettes and rotten food. Everywhere they looked they saw piles of rubbish, empty beer cans and dirty clothing scattered over the chairs, tables and counter space.

"At the very least he's blown his chance for any Good Housekeeping awards," said Jake.

"Now don't rush to conclusions, we haven't seen the rest of the trailer," replied Reed as he paused to look at the images on the computer screen. "On second thought, perhaps the good Mr. Salvaggio may have some other issues that we need to examine. It seems that he has an interest in kiddy porn according to what's on the screen."

Jake walked over, glanced at the screen, and replied, "I suggest we take 'good ole' Mr. Salvaggio for a ride after we read him his rights. Then we can come back with a warrant and see just how bad of a boy we have here. I don't know if there's any connection to the Mortenson girl but at the very least we need to have his computer scrutinized."

"I'm with ya', Jake, but I wouldn't bet on him being the killer. It generally doesn't fit the profile," said Reed as he pulled the front door closed and headed for the car.

The male beagle, who had been so noisy on their arrival, was preoccupied licking his genitalia as the men walked past.

"You know," offered Jake. "I wish that I could do that."

"Probably if you pat him nicely, he'll let you," replied Reed without the hint of a grin.

~ 15 ~

After it had been determined that the note fastened to the body of Carrie Mortenson was in the same handwriting as the first murder, and the knife was that which was missing from the set in Gorham, Reed made the decision to add another detective to the case as a secondary. It was Reed's feeling that Walt Wizkowski was the ideal candidate for such an assignment. Jake, who had been earlier given the case of Angela Carrington, would remain the "primary' in what now appeared to be the work of a serial killer. As usual, the rest of the detectives assigned to the Southern Division would also be involved.

For two days the MSP detectives, as well as the local police, had analyzed, examined and postulated on how and what had occurred. They had re-enacted the crime, collected dozens of bits of bark, twigs and leaves in the hopes that they would provide some information and they had interviewed hundreds of students who lived, or were engaged in activities, near the crime scene.

A command post was established in the Brunswick Police Department and a conference room had been commandeered to display bits of evidence, photographs and house the many meetings that may be needed to discuss and disseminate information until the activity would return to Gray.

Such was the case as Reed, Jake, Walt Wizkowski, Tom Lombardo, Frank Durgin, Bruce Costello and Joe Quinn sat around two long tables along with several Brunswick cops including Tim Stockwell and the Chief of Police, Mack Rollins. Walker Gray was also invited to sit in on the briefing.

"Gentleman," began Reed, bringing the many side conversations to a halt. "What we have here is a serious and potentially volatile situation as it relates to the Bowdoin campus, the media, and the community at large. I cannot stress enough the need to keep the information discussed today 'in house.' We do not need hysteria in public or on Maine's college campuses. For obvious reasons we will withhold some information from the masses including the presence and contents of the note. All information will be disseminated through my office. Having said that, what do we know?"

Jake was the first to respond. "A 20 year old sophomore, Carrie Mortenson from Reading, Mass., goes out for an afternoon jog, is surprised en route and killed. The perpetrator used a serrated knife, the same one used on Angela Carrington, and stabbed her multiple times. He penetrated both of her lungs as well as her heart. Post mortem he cut off her right hand at the wrist. and then moved her body some 25 feet off the jogging path and leaned her up against a pine tree. He then drove the knife into her once more to hold the note that he left at the scene."

"What about the time frame?" asked Reed.

"The ME placed the time of death between 4:00 and 7:00 Saturday evening. This fits, according to her roommate, Hannah Parisi, who said Carrie went out for a run sometime after 4:00."

"Was the crime lab able to identify any discernable evidence at the scene?" asked Joe Quinn, a detective who looked more like a movie star than a cop with a rock hard chin, two pronounced dimples and short dark hair turning gray around his ears.

Jake, as the primary, fielded the question. "There was a lot of blood at the scene but it appears that it all belongs to the victim. The only exception to that is the blood used to paint the message. The lab says that it matches that of Angela Carrington."

"You mean the killer took blood from his first crime scene to leave a message at the second," asked Tim Stockwell.

"It appears that way Tim," said Jake, as he continued on with information from his report.

"We did find a cigarette butt near the scene and are having it checked for DNA but there's no assurance it belongs to the perp – it looked too old. We've also made literally dozens of footprints casts, but because it is a heavily traveled pathway we have no way of knowing whose belong to whom."

"Why would the bastard cut off her hand?" asked one of the Brunswick patrolmen

"Let me handle this one, Jake," offered Reed, as he lifted his left leg into one of the folding chairs. "He removed a breast from the girl killed in Gorham so it may be that he wants a souvenir or we think there may have been a scuffle and perhaps she scratched him. The unsub, recognizing this, cut off her hand to eliminate any DNA being discovered under her fingernails. Don't underestimate this guy – he's obviously very bright … and very careful."

"If he's so god damn careful," asked Bruce Costello, a thirty year veteran of the MSP, "then why would he attack a co-ed in broad daylight where he could be seen?"

"Perhaps he's familiar with the area or perhaps he knew the victim so she stopped to speak with him," suggested Tom Lombardo, one hand curling his handlebar mustache with his thumb and index finger.

"We've thought of that angle, Guy," said Reed, using the common nickname given to the heavy detective. "But rather than an absence of activity, which would be the case if she knew him, the crime scene appeared to have been 'tidied up' as if there was a struggle and it was swirled clean with a branch. We found pine needles and dirt in a circular pattern and even from the path to the tree, where she was placed, there was a smooth surface… probably an attempt to cover his footprints. We know he wore gloves since there were no prints on the knife."

"What I don't get," said Tim Stockwell, "is why he bothered to move her from the running path. Why go to the effort of posing the girl?"

"Our perp is sure of himself," answered Reed. "By putting the girls on display he is taunting us, letting us know that he is smarter than we are. He took the time to paint a message on the wall in Gorham and took the time to pose her there as well. It shows that he *knows* the habits and patterns of these girls and is unafraid and unaffected by what goes on around them. The fact that there was no sign of forced entry in Gorham and that he knew when and where to be waiting for Carrie Mortenson tells us that these are not random acts of violence, gentlemen. Our boy has planned these acts carefully. It certainly appears that he had been stalking them."

~ 16 ~

"Hey, Reed. What about the maintenance guy that you and Jake checked out?" asked Walker Gray. "The guy we let go."

Reed responded, "We got a warrant, confiscated his computer, and have had the boys in the lab go through it. It seems that Mr. Salvaggio has an affinity for young boys. He has been charged with possession of pornographic images of children and released on bail but unfortunately for us he has a solid alibi. The computer shows that he was logged onto 'Troubled Teens' during the time of the murder. He may be a sicko but it doesn't look like he's our murderer. His profile just doesn't fit the crimes."

Reed continued with the briefing asking the Brunswick Police Chief, "Mack, your men interviewed a great many students – any leads?"

"We have the girl being seen running both on Longfellow Ave and Harpswell Road but nothing after that. Nobody saw anyone running with, or near her, nor anyone suspicious looking as she ran by. As you guys know, kids don't pay attention anyway."

Frank Durgin spoke up, "I interviewed Sam Magee who, up to about three weeks ago, was dating Carrie. He said that he had run with her on several occasions and that she always went the same way and if she wanted to go for a longer run she would re-trace her route. It's as you suggested, someone knew her pattern."

"Thank you, Frank. Anything else?"

"Only that Sam Magee said that he was studying with several other students during the time in question and it was confirmed."

Reed walked over to a white, dry-erase board in the corner of the room and turned it slightly so all could see the enlarged copies of the two notes left at the crime scenes.

"This leaves us with perhaps our best clues, yet biggest mysteries – the messages - another opportunity for him to tell us, *show us,* that he's in control." The group stared at the new note, many seeing it for the first time.

41

Wonderment seizes everyone
awaken to the glory be
the child has sanctums
irenic will never see

Once again, Walt Wizkowski was singled out by Reed. "Wiz, you have spent a lot of time studying these. Have you made any progress? Have you been able to decipher anything?"

"A couple of things can clearly be drawn from these messages," he began, "and that is, whoever is doing the killing is very well read and has a large vocabulary – sanctums and irenic are not words in most people's vocabulary."

"Certainly not in most cop's anyway," chimed in Tom Lombardo, which was quickly agreed to by many.

"The word 'wonderment' tends to imply awe. The second line reflects the 72nd Psalm, 'when the sleeper awakes Glory Be to the Father and to the Son and to the Holy Spirit.' 'Sanctum' is a sacred or holy place, a place free from intrusion. Finally, 'irenic' means peaceful or promoting peace."

"Hell, it's an early Christmas card," said Lombardo, causing a good deal of commotion.

"So Wiz," began Reed, trying to bring the group back on task. "What conclusions can you draw from the note if any?"

"It seems that he is describing a scene of serenity and peace – perhaps he feels the act of killing is taking the victims to a better place. By drawing from the Bible and describing a location as sacred and using the term 'wonderment', as opposed to 'wonder' or 'wonderful' it suggests that he may believe that he, or his actions, are God-like. In a way it ties in with the first note where there also was a religious tone."

"I don't see it – how is slaughtering a young girl God-like?" asked Frank Durgin.

"In his eyes, Frank," answered Reed, drawing upon his earlier days as a psychoanalyst, "killers see their actions as cleansing, what is referred to as 'missionary killing.' While he may recognize that his act is wrong he has such little value for human life that he feels he is actually helping society. We have seen this on many occasions with serial killers who have chosen an isolated group such as prostitutes or homosexuals."

"How does that relate to these two girls," asked Bruce Costello, a red-haired detective with a face full of freckles and hands the size of ping-pong paddles.

Reed continued. "That's what we're not sure of but perhaps it's a physical attribute. Many serial killers devise motives predicated on earlier tribulations or attractions. Ted Bundy killed women with straight hair parted in the middle while Ramiro Artieda killed women who resembled his fiancé who jilted him. Remember Wayne Williams who killed so many black children in Atlanta? …. Tom, for that reason I'd like you to closely examine physical similarities between the girls. Compare facial features, hair style and color … had either of them dyed their hair recently? … measurements, dress patterns, etcetera."

"Bruce, I'd like you to examine if they frequented any of the same clubs, gyms, stores or businesses. It's not uncommon for serial killers to frequent a particular type of location like a shopping mall, woods, or college campus. Pedro Lopez, who was responsible for over one hundred murders in South America, chose young girls from the market places of Peru. That is what we need to find - some commonality. Obviously the fact that both of the victims were college students is a start. What we don't know is why *these two* and why on college campuses some forty miles apart?"

"Wiz, you keep working on the notes. We're definitely missing something."

~ 17 ~

"Good job, Tommy, but remember, look right, left, right before taking that left turn."

"I thought I did, Dad,"

"I didn't see you look back. You know they'll be looking for that when you go for your license."

Tommy drove carefully, though perhaps not confidently, down Lejok Street, turned right on High and headed west toward the outskirts of town. Reed turned on the radio to 99.9 'The Wolf" and hummed along with Steve Holy as he got 'A brand new girl friend.'

In order to get the 60 hours of supervised driving required while on his permit Tommy would beg his dad to let him drive whenever he was home. Reed tried to acquiesce. While his mind was most often miles away buried in whatever case he was working on at the time it did allow him "quality" time with his eldest son. On this occasion, they were using Jake's white Toyota Camry while Jake was using their Explorer to move some furniture for his sister.

He looked across at the driver's side and felt a sense of pride swell within him. Tommy had recently gone through one of his growth spurts and, at 16, was almost as tall as his father. He looks more like me every day, thought Reed. If I could just get him to stop wearing that damn Yankees cap. Ah, the independence of youth.

Neither of them noticed the black SUV that had stealthily come up behind them. As Tommy slowed to a stop at the corner of High Street and Warren Avenue the SUV pulled alongside their car and three blasts from a handgun resounded through the morning air.

Reed screamed, "GOD NO!! before slamming the stick shift into park. He made a mental note of the small decal on the rear window – "Five Words" - as it sped away. He also noticed that the Cadillac Escalade had no rear license plate. Reed saw

Tommy's body go limp and his head fall forward into the steering wheel. Blood dripped from his ear and out of his mouth onto his dad's sleeve.

Reed woke with a start, damp sweat oozing from every pore of his body. His top sheet, cold and clammy had been pulled loose and was wrapped around his neck. The rest of the bed resembled a crime scene with pillows on the floor, blankets bunched into a pile. He rubbed his eyes and looked at the alarm clock on the dresser beside his bed. The clock glowed 3:40 in red-lined digits. *These are the times I feel so alone,* he thought.

He got up and threw on his navy blue, terry cloth robe. After a visit to the bathroom he walked down the hall to make sure Scott was safe. Barney's tail slapped the bed covers as Reed ran his hand through Scott's hair and looked deep into his face. When Scott began to stir Reed backed away. He could hear Sandy snoring from across the hall as he walked back into his room and reached for the phone.

Amy picked up on the third ring knowing full well who it was. "Tough night?" she answered.

"Yea, same dream. Sorry I called this time of night but I knew you'd understand."

"I understand only too well, Reed. It's a pain I live with every day."

"I miss you Amy"

"I miss you too, Reed, and I miss Tommy. I miss seeing his smile when he played a trick on Scott, his alarm over the first pimple on his forehead, his fear in asking Alyssa Watkins to the middle school dance, his jubilation at getting his permit" - she was crying now. "I miss seeing him as he grew into a smaller version of you, tough and proud and tender. I cannot get him back, Reed. I can't stand knowing that."

Reed rubbed his right eye with his knuckle. "I know, Amy. I feel the same way. Can you imagine what it's like seeing our son being shot - dying in my arms - having his last words be 'I love you, Dad.'" Reed fought to hold back the tears forming in his eyes but he was losing the battle.

"Amy, can … we get together for dinner?"

"Call me later this morning."

"I will … and thanks."

~ 18 ~

The Painter was growing anxious. He had consumed a baloney sandwich and several cups of coffee but it wasn't the caffeine that had him on edge - it was the anticipation of the next victim, the next kill! Like a rogue lion prowling the plains in search of the weakest link in the herd he was alert and alive. Unlike the lion, this wouldn't be random.

He knew who he was to kill. He had been instructed by 'The Voice' who his next victim was to be and now he only had to use his superior intellect to determine "the when," "the where," and "the how" – the particulars, the delicious specifics that he alone would bring to the job. Today was the day he had decided upon for his next "event" and all of the particulars had been worked out in his mind.

It has been said that, "the Devil is in the details" and oh, how he loved the details. He had watched the girl for days. He observed her going to school, watched as she worked out at The Fitness Barn and had even followed her as she walked the aisles of Hannaford's grocery store shopping for food. He knew how many minutes she tanned on Tuesdays and Thursdays at The Sun Deck, knew her baby-sitting routine on the weekend and even knew what her favorite parking place had been with her boyfriend, a grease monkey named Brandon Hancock, who she had only recently broken up with. She was bright, she was pretty, she was athletic, but most importantly - she was next!

He sat in his white van and took a sip from his coffee. *Blinded by the Light* was on the radio…. killing was on his mind!

~ 19 ~

Deanna Porter walked out the back door of Windham High School into the parking lot. She clicked the button on her key chain and the lights on her 2000 Honda Accord flicked on. It had been a spirited cheerleading practice but she was anxious to get home. She tucked her short blonde hair under the hood of her gray Converse sweat shirt and walked toward her car.

In her navy blue Nike sweat pants and white Reebok footwear she looked like the All-American girl. She didn't see any reason why the Eagles wouldn't win on Friday night. Nor did she see the man sitting in the white van three parking spots away.

Deanna started her car, put in her favorite CD, Colbie Caillat's *Coco,* and pulled out of the parking lot. She headed out the back way down the Windham Center Road and then she remembered that her father was away on business and she needed to stop and get milk and bread before going home.

Ever since her mother died, when she was fourteen, she had been doing much of the shopping for her and her father but Deanna didn't mind. It was the least that she could do. She pulled into Patches, a 'mom and pop' store, picked up the necessary few items, and then headed for home.

As she put the key in the lock she noticed that her pet basset hound, Josie, was not barking as she normally did when someone came to the door. Stepping into the mud room she reached for the light but her hand never reached its destination. Instead, her arm was grabbed, pulled inside behind her back and a hand was placed roughly over her mouth.

"Hello, Deanna," she heard a male voice whisper into her ear. "I've been looking forward to meeting you in person."

The bag of groceries fell out of Deanna's other arm as she tried to comprehend what was occurring. Fear swelled within her as she struggled to catch her breath. His warm breath on the back of her neck caused her hairs to stand up. Tears welled in her eyes as his grip on her tightened.

"I'm going to remove my hand from your mouth but if you scream I'm going to have to hurt you," he said to her as he reached into his pocket. Withdrawing a roll of gray duct tape, he extended his arms to eye-measure the necessary length and then tore off a piece that long. The Painter then placed the tape over the girl's mouth running almost from ear to ear. "Now, now, Dear, there's no need to cry," he said, rubbing his hand over her cheek and then through her hair. "This will be over soon."

He lifted the sweatshirt over her head, pulled both arms behind her back and made a series of loops around her wrists and then did the same thing to her ankles. He removed her cheering shoes and then guided her as she hobbled through the kitchen and into the living room where he pushed her onto the brown leather sofa.

Deanna whimpered into the tape as she watched the man reach into his gray overalls and remove a pair of white latex gloves which he slid on over his hands like a surgeon preparing for an operation. Next, he produced a large hunting knife held in a leather sheath. He unhooked the knife and held it up in front of his face as he rubbed his thumb against the razor-sharp blade. Deanna briefly saw her own reflection in the blade and the severity of her situation swept through her causing her to tremble. Finally, he withdrew a thin synthetic brush, the type she remembered using when she stained her book shelf with Minwax earlier that week. He put the two items on the coffee table in front of her.

Deanna watched the man walk over to the entrance to the upstairs which was hidden behind a wall covered with family photos and memorabilia. Her eyes filled with tears as she saw him throw framed pictures and certificates onto the fireplace hearth in front of her. There was the photo of her and her mother at her 13th birthday party - the last photo with her mother before she succumbed to cancer. Although it was over five years ago, Deanna remembered fondly the "You're now a teen-ager party" that her parents threw for her and the photo showed a proud mother standing behind the young girl as she blew out the candles on her birthday cake.

"What a happy little family, Deanna. And look at all of your accomplishments. Why you've been such a joy to your father. I'll bet he is so proud of you."

The Painter continued to remove ribbons, certificates, and family photos from the wall and throw them onto the brick surface where they lay shredded and shattered. All remembrances of happy times in rural America; Rockwellian capsules captured in time.

Finally, the wall was void of all items. *My canvas is now clear,* he thought - *all that is needed is the paint!*

~ 20 ~

The Painter walked over to the terrified girl who tried to shrink into the sofa away from the man. She tried to study his features noting his shaggy dark hair, eyes as black and stagnant as manhole covers and a scar the shape of a crescent moon that ran from his left eye down past his mouth.

"You're such a pretty little thing. Let's see what we have under all this clothing." He picked up the knife and while he held her maroon and white t-shirt in his left hand he made one swift downward stroke slicing the shirt in half lengthways. He did the same with the elastic center of her bra and then pulled both items away from her body. His glove-covered hands took one breast in each hand, lifting and stroking her flesh.

Deanna tried to wriggle away from his fondling but only managed to fall down sideways on the sofa landing on her side. As she lie there her eyes were drawn to a lifeless form of brown, black and white surrounded by liquid beside the La - Z - Boy recliner. She recoiled as she recognized her basset hound Josie, eyes vacant, her throat cut. She tried to summon the strength to tear the tape on both her wrists and ankles but only managed to tire herself out and create more tension which cut into her skin.

The Painter lifted her into an upright position. "Where do you think you're going, my little pet? There's no one who can save you so you might just as well relax. Daddy Wayne is out of town on business and isn't it a shame that you broke up with Brandon last week. If only you had let him screw you then perhaps you wouldn't be in this dilemma, although I did enjoy watching you blow him up on The Bluff."

How in the world did he know her dad's name or that he was out of town on business, she thought, *and how in hell did he know about Brandon.* It was true, her ex-boyfriend, who was three years older than her, had been pressuring her to "go all the way" but she was not ready for that with Brandon? It was not that she was a virgin, that had been taken care of two years earlier at Camp Mineotka where she worked as a counselor, but she just wasn't sure about Brandon so she had used other methods to keep him satisfied.

"Oh yes," he continued, running his hand through her hair and gently across her cheek. "I know all your little secrets, your habits and your interests. You see, you and I have had a date with destiny for a long time. You just didn't know it. I have learned a great deal about you and have so been looking forward to this day. I would really like to sit and chat with you but I have to paint a message for those who will find you and you are going to help me."

Deanna had no idea what this demented bastard was talking about but the intent was clear. She tried to withdraw into the cushions of the couch, away from him, but it was to no avail. A feeling of helplessness swept over her as he reached for her again.

~ 21 ~

The Painter leaned in on the girl as if to nuzzle into her neck. His hands went to the sides of her sweat pants and with one quick tug they slid down over her buttocks and thighs and lay bunched against the tape of her ankles. He then enlisted the knife to cut the inseam of the pants on both sides and slid them around her ankles onto the floor.

"What a purty little pink thong," he said as he rubbed his gloved hand between her legs. He then cut the thin strap on the side of her underwear on both sides, pulled it from underneath her and chuckled, "I'll bet ole Brandon would like to see you now Deanna. Do you find it ironic that he spent over a year trying to get into your pants and here I am playing with you on our first date?"

Any sense of embarrassment that Deanna felt was shrouded by the fear that engulfed her. She tried to plead but the tape prohibited everything but muffled whimpers. He looked into her baleful eyes but was not ready for what happened next. She leaned back, brought her knees up to her chest and lunged forward with both feet driving her heels into the man's groin. He yelped in pain as he fell backwards over the coffee table, his extended arm slamming against the brick corners of the fireplace hearth.

She rose to her stockinged feet and tried to move across the living room and into the kitchen but he was on her before she crossed under the arch. His right hand grabbed her by the hair, yanking her back off her feet. Angrily he slapped her across her face, bringing stars to her eyes. "You fucking bitch," he sputtered. "I'm all done playing with you."

She could see he had blood on the back of his hand in a tear to the glove where he fell into the shattered picture frames on the hearth. His eyes had taken on a glazed look.

He grabbed a chair from the kitchen and put it in front of the wall where the pictures had once been hung. With one hand under her arm and the other grabbing her by the hair he pulled her up and threw her into the chair. He then grabbed the roll of duct tape and slapped it on her stomach making several passes around the back of the kitchen chair each tighter than the one before. "That ought to hold you, ya' little cock-tease."

The man then walked into the kitchen, came back with another chair which he put beside the one holding Deanna, and picked up the brush which was on the floor. His knife, also, was on the floor where it had landed when he had fallen. He picked it up, removed a hand-written note from his left pocket, and sat down beside the girl, a crazed smile firmly entrenched on his face.

Gently removing strands of hair and wiping tears from her eyes he whispered, "What say you and I paint a picture, little darlin'."

The Painter's first cut was purposely superficial. The next several were not.

~ 22 ~

Reed was working in his office when Jake walked in and sat down in the leather chair facing his desk. "Ya' gotta minute?" he asked.

"Sure," Reed replied. "What's on your mind?"

"Tommy. I know we have been absorbed in the recent murders of the girls but a day does not go by that I don't think about your son."

"Jake listen. We have been through this before and it was not your fault that Tommy was killed."

"I know you say that but if he wasn't driving my car then he wouldn't have been shot."

"You don't know that."

"I am convinced of that. You remember telling me that you saw a small bumper sticker or decal in the window of the shooter's car - 'Five Words.'"

"Yea"

"Well, I've done a lot of work on that and I'm convinced that it goes back to my involvement with hate crimes and the KKK coming back to Maine."

"I'm not sure it ever left."

"No, but you know what I mean. Remember a few years back there was a KKK rally in Rumford and more recently a Wisconsin KKK group paraded against Somalis in Lewiston which led to a confrontation."

"I remember. What's your point?"

"I was called in to help maintain peace in that city and wound up getting in a skirmish with a couple of Klan members. I threw one of them up against a car and he later died."

"But that wasn't your fault. He had a heart attack."

"I know that and you know that but I'm not so sure the boys with white hoods have such a positive appreciation of my involvement."

"What does that have to do with the 'Five Words' bumper sticker?"

Jake got up from his chair and stood looking out into the reception area. "In 2003, a white supremacist named Metzger presented a plan for action at a rally in Indiana. His concept calls for skinheads and supremacists to become less visible and blend in more with the mainstream society even while committing heinous acts against minorities. It was in that presentation that he coined the phrase 'Five Words' which translates to 'I have nothing to say' if one is caught in the commission of an illegal act. I believe the SUV with the bumper sticker you saw belongs to a skinhead who may have been trying to get back at me for my involvement in that guys death. I'm guessing that he, or they, may have been planning this drive-by and had no idea that you or Tommy were using my car."

Reed put his feet up on the corner of his desk before replying. "You're making an awful lot of assumptions here aren't you. Since that rally in Lewiston and the reporting of KKK writings along that walking trail in Hallowell, we really haven't seen much hate crime activity up here."

"No, we're fortunate, but it's not like it doesn't exist. In the 1920's there were 150,000 Klan members in Maine alone but now it is more likely to be individuals who are part of a splinter group. I don't think that bumper sticker was purely coincidental Reed, I'll keep digging and we *will* catch that bastard."

"I hope you're right, Jake. I think of Tommy constantly just like I think of the girls who have been murdered. I know how their parents feel and it leaves a constant ache deep inside my gut. It drives me to want to find the answers."

Reed looked down at the paperwork on his desk, a compilation of all the Cadillacs sold in Maine since 1999, the year the Escalade was introduced, and said, "Say, I've got several calls I need to make. How 'bout we have a beer a little later?"

"Sounds good. I'll meet you at Jimmy D's"

"Oh, one more thing, Jake. If it is like you say, then whoever tried to kill you probably knows where you live and since they were unsuccessful they may try again. I'd be especially careful if I was you."

~ 23 ~

The Painter left the Porter house and walked slowly down the driveway toward his van. An orange harvest moon was climbing above the tree line in front of him bringing an autumnal radiance to the darkness. When he reached the street he turned right and walked several hundred feet to where he had carefully chosen to park. He glanced in all directions and when he was sure that no one had been watching him he climbed into the van. Cursing, he looked at the small cut on his hand where he had landed on the broken picture frames.

Beside the seat was a small canvas bag in which he placed the knife, the paint brush, the duct tape and the plastic gloves as he had been instructed. He also carefully removed from his pocket several pieces of broken glass from the broken picture frames and a handful of shards that had his blood on them and placed them in the bag.

Turning the key he peered into the rear view mirror. No cars appeared in his view but he was drawn to his face with the deep scar which ran from his left eye down his cheek to his chin; the result of a beer bottle that had been broken against the side of his face some years ago. It caused his eye to droop and greatly impaired his vision. He understood that people were repulsed when they looked at him but he didn't care. With a knife in his hand, it was HE that was in control and as long as 'The Voice' was pleased with his work, that was all that mattered.

He drove the fifteen minutes home, went slowly down the long winding dirt road and carefully pulled his van into the dilapidated garage. After he fastened and locked the old wooden door, he grabbed the bag from the front seat and entered the farmhouse through the basement bulkhead. He took his hand and rubbed the cobwebs out of his hair after walking through a large spider's web and placed the canvas bag with the contents of the Porter house on the floor at the base of the stairs. He continued on through a damp, musty corridor until he reached a room on the left.

He removed an open padlock, lifted the latch, returned the lock to its original position and stepped into the eight foot square space. He removed his clothing and hung the items on a spike driven into one of the stones that formed a wall. After relieving himself in a white plastic bucket The Painter placed a thin black hood onto his head. He turned on a small electric space heater, lied down on the mattress and pulled the hood down around his neck.

He was home.

~ 24 ~

Jimmy D's is a bar the likes of which are in every city in America. It contained a modicum of sports memorabilia, in this case with an emphasis on the revered Boston Red Sox. There was dusty faux Tiffany lighting turned low, dark wood booths ideal for commiserations or confessions, and a short namesake bartender whose smile came as quickly and as often as the "on the house" shots for his regulars. It served greasy food that the regulars raved about, but no Cosmopolitans or blender drinks. As Jimmy was fond of saying, 'If you want Sex-on-the-beach - go to Old Orchard.' There was only seating for a couple of dozen, so the place was usually crowded and the belly-up-to-the-bar conversation tended to be animated and revolve around local sports and politics.

More of a neighborhood bar than a destination location, it attracted its share of Runyanesque characters; locals looking for "a quick beer," or "last call" regardless of the time of day. It was a favorite hangout for many of the local cops and Reed often stopped in here on his way home, more so since Amy had moved out.

"Hey, Jimmy, what's up?"

"Gas prices and Paul Pierce's scoring average," he replied, an ever-present white dish rag hanging from his left shoulder matching the color of his sparse hair. "What can I get ya?"

"Gimme a CC and ginger Jim. Say, has Jake been in?"

"Down back, … just got here actually. Have a seat. I'll bring that over to you."

Reed sat down opposite Jake in the booth and put his elbow on the table between them as if to arm wrestle. "C'mon Pat Benatar. Hit me with your best shot."

Jake leaned his massive frame into the table, dwarfed Reed's hand and arm with his own, and then proceeded to feign a quick defeat, the back of his hand touching the table.

"I give, Reedie. You da' man."

"As expected. How 'bout I buy you a spinach quiche and a

Shirley Temple?"

Jimmy appeared setting Reed's drink in front of him and a draft beer in front of Jake beside his near-empty bottle.

"Thanks, Jimmy, How'd you' know?"

"Lucky guess, Jake."

Each took a long drag from their drink before Jake spoke.

"How's things at home - any better?"

"Nah, about the same. I'm hoping to have Amy over the house for dinner but with this killer out there I don't know when I'll have time. I'm afraid we've got a real psycho on our hands this time. We haven't seen anything in Maine like this in years."

"Do we know any more?"

"We have a real pro here, Jake. He hasn't left finger or footprints, only notes which make little sense, yet must be at the heart of the matter. He's obviously bright and he's taunting us. Remember the Zodiac killer out in California and the BTK killer in Wichita. Both of them sent clues to the newspaper as well as to the police. We've had one girl killed in Gorham, one in Brunswick. One had blonde hair, the other dark. One was a junior in college, one a sophomore. One was killed inside, one outside. In both instances a knife was used but in the first he used a knife on site and in the second he brings the knife with him. It appears that the killer may be evolving. The constant is that they're both college students and at both scenes a note was left. We've got to solve those notes, Jake or I'm afraid the body count will rise."

"We will, Reed. Sooner or later he'll make a mistake and we'll get the son of a bitch. Still nothing from the lab?"

"Not a thing of any value. He's a careful bastard."

Jake wiped beer foam from his mouth with the back of his meaty hand. "How about the notes. Do we know anymore?"

"I'm afraid not. If we can't make any headway in the next few days then I am going to send what we have to the Feds at Quantico and see if their cryptology people can provide any answers."

As he ran his hands through his hair he saw Susan walking towards their booth.

"Hey, guys, buy a girl a drink?"

"I'm sure that Reed will be glad to," said Jake as he slid out of the booth and stood up. But I have to run."

"That'll be a first," said Reed.

"You know what I mean. Here, Susan, you can be the relief pitcher for this game. Rest assured that I turned in another quality start. I'll see you both later."

Jimmy appeared and took Susan's drink order and quickly returned with that and a refill for Reed.

"What brings you out tonight Susan?"

"I guess, like you, the death of these girls is getting to me, and thought maybe a cocktail might help me unwind. Liz is spending the night at a friend's house," replied Susan, referring to her daughter.

"Does she know about the murders?"

"It's all over the television so like most people she knows what's been released. She asked me a couple of questions but I didn't tell her much. I'd rather she not know all the grisly details. They're all scared enough as it is."

Reed rubbed his eyes with the knuckles of his index fingers and sighed, "There's got to be a motive behind these killings because he wouldn't leave notes if he didn't want us to 'play along.' He is obviously cocksure of himself. There have been virtually no other clues left behind … if only we could understand the messages."

"How are you doing, Reed?"

"Not very well, there just isn't much to go on."

"No, I mean how are *you* doing?"

"Okay, thanks Susan. I'm getting tired like everyone involved in the case, but I'm fine." Susan leaned forward in the booth allowing Reed a full view of her cleavage. He felt her leg rest against his under the table but chose not to do anything about it. He thought about how long it had been since he had been with a woman.

"I know it's been difficult for you since Amy left. Plus, with this case weighing on you, I thought you might like some female companionship."

Reed inhaled deeply as his eyes absorbed Susan's breasts and noticed that she wasn't wearing a bra. She observed this, discreetly released another button so the full scope of her chest could be seen and then reached in with her left hand to cup her right breast.

Reed felt a stirring in his trousers as she squeezed her nipple between her index finger and thumb and although he knew he should resist he heard himself say, "I'll meet you at your place."

Reed made the short drive to her place and when he walked in the door he was greeted by Susan who was now wearing a low-cut black negligee. She handed him a whiskey and ginger saying, "The price is right and the service better."

"I have no doubts," agreed Reed as he followed her to the sofa. Nora Jones' *Come away with me* played in the background as two pine-scented candles flickered softly in the darkened room casting shadows against the living room walls.

Susan took a long draft from her drink and then placed it on the end table beside her. She reached for Reed's drink, took it out of his hand, and put it beside hers. She then placed her hand on his neck and pulled him to her, their mouths interlocking in a feverish kiss.

Reed leaned down lowering his body to meet hers and felt Susan's fingernails press against the inside of his knee moving upward. He felt himself grow hard as his right hand reached inside her chemise gently cupping her left breast. Their breathing was labored as their tongues explored the other's mouth. Susan's hand was now tracing Reed's manhood, squeezing and rubbing his erection to full length. She began to slide his zipper down when Reed's mouth broke from hers.

"Susan… wait!"

"What's the matter?"

"Nothing .. It's just, … that I can't do this."

"Baby, you know that you want to … we both need it. Look how hard you are."

"I'm sorry, Susan. There's no question that I'm horny … but I can't do this to Amy."

"Reed, she left you! She's not thinking about what's best for you. She doesn't care where you are tonight."

"That may be true but I am still married. As much as I would like to go to bed with you I just can't do it. I am sorry. It's best that I go now."

Susan stood as Reed rose from the couch pulled up his zipper and rearranged his clothing. He gave her a quick kiss on the cheek, squeezed her hand and then headed for the door. "I *am* sorry," he repeated softly as he turned the handle on the front door and looked back at her.

Susan watched as his car backed down the driveway and out of her yard, tears of frustration forming in her eyes.

Reed made the short drive to his house, his mind swirling with a myriad of mixed emotions. When he arrived home he walked straight into Scott's room, stood beside his bed and listened to him breathe. Barney, who was lying at the end of the bed, looked up as Reed reached down to gently run his fingers through his son's hair, causing all feelings of ambivalence to be erased.

~ 25 ~

Reed rolled over in bed and pulled the blankets up around his neck. His late arrival home last night, long after everyone had gone to bed, had become the norm ever since The Painter had made Angela Carrington his first victim.

He thought he heard voices coming from the kitchen but when he glanced at the alarm clock beside his bed he saw that it read 6:25. While it might not be unusual for Sandy to be up at this time, he knew that it would be a long time before Scott would greet the world – especially on a weekend. Probably Sandy listening to the news, he thought, as he buried his head under a pillow.

He wasn't sure what to think when moments later his door opened and in walked both Sandy and Scott. The former had the morning's edition of the Portland Press Herald and the latter a tray of food complete with orange juice, fried eggs and bacon and a cup of International Foods Orange Cappuccino coffee.

"Time to get up, Sport," said Sandy. "There's only one type of person that can make money in bed and me-thinks we'd be starving if we were relying on you for that."

"Morning, Dad," beamed Scott. "We thought as hard as you have been working, you deserved breakfast in bed." He placed the tray down on the end of his father's bed.

Reed rubbed the sleep from his eyes and sat up pulling the tray over his lap. "Wow, you guys didn't have to do this but I really appreciate it." "I made the eggs just the way you like them, Dad – over medium."

"They're perfect Scotty – thank you both … and Sandy, as for your comment about making money, me-thinks that if it was the case this place would be like a deli – they'd be forced to get in line and take a number."

Sandy said nothing but a smile covered his face as he headed back into the kitchen. Scott climbed up onto the foot of the bed as his dad cut his eggs with a fork.

Looking up Reed stared deeply into his son's eyes. "You know Scott, I don't say this nearly often enough but I really do love you."

Scott matched his father's stare and appreciation of the moment. "I know you do Dad, and I love you, too. With all my heart."

~ 26 ~

The Painter could hear the footsteps coming down the wooden stairs. Although he had no idea what time it was or how long he had been lying on his mattress, he knew he would soon get a "treat."

He heard the lock being played with, the rusty squeak of the heavy wooden door and the familiar metallic clang of his food bowl being placed on the hard dirt floor. Next came a click and he knew the small television against the wall had been turned on. Although he could not distinguish sights or shapes he could "see" the difference in lighting through his dark hood.

Soon he would remove his covering so that he could look at what was on the screen but first he knew that he must wait for the tell-tale sound of his padlock being fastened. As the footsteps disappeared down the hall and then back up the stairs, The Painter removed his hood and stared at the screen which showed naked bodies engaged in sexual activity. He chose to ignore that and instead reached into his bowl, removed a handful of food, and leaned back on his haunches as he brought it to his mouth. He relished his treats.

The Painter had been taught that he was to once again fasten his hood and tie it with the yarn that hung from both sides of his mouth. It restricted his air marginally but, more importantly, it held the covering securely around his neck. He once again heard footsteps coming down the stairs. The lock outside his room was undone and he sensed the presence of another in his room. He pulled down his underwear as he had been taught many years ago and stood rock solid, his legs spread shoulder width apart.

A hand reached out cupping his scrotum and pulled, bringing tears to his eyes. He felt his penis getting longer despite his willing, no praying, for it not to, muffled sounds of feigned pleasure emanating from the television nearby. 'The Voice' spoke softly, resolutely, "this is your time, your opportunity to play with yourself. You know you want to – all guys love to play with their things. Now, I'm going to stay right here until you are done."

~ 27 ~

WINDHAM GIRL MURDERED
"THE PAINTER" STRIKES AGAIN

The front page of the Portland Press Herald, Maine's largest daily, screamed the news that people didn't want to read.

Reed didn't need to read the morning paper to be appraised of the situation in Windham. In fact, he had arrived on the scene long before the papers had been delivered. Again, he was sickened by the wanton and senseless act.

As he looked out the window of the Porter's house he could see the television stations mobile units vying for position. Lisa Landsburg and other anchors were trying to glean bits of information and interviews from beat cops as well as anyone who had witnessed the crime scene.

Windham police had kept all media from entering the driveway and already the yard was full of unmarked cars, cruisers, and emergency vehicles. Reed shuddered at the thought of how much play this would get. By dinner time citizens from Alfred to Allagash would know that yet another murder had been committed and rumors would be flying that the State truly did have a serial killer on its hands.

Deanna Porter's body was found with her face pushed into the leather couch, her arms extended underneath. Her legs hung over the thick arm rests, her buttocks arched toward the ceiling. On each side the killer had cut a portion of her buttocks off and these were absent from the scene.

"Jesus Christ, Reed," said Jake. "He filleted her like a piece of flank steak. Just how sick is this bastard?"

"He's evolving," Reed replied. "He dehumanizes them after torturing them. He is a sexual sadist who gets great satisfaction from his inter-actions with the victims. Looking at the amount of blood at the scene it is my belief that he cut the girl and had her watch, her life ebbing away, as he painted his message on the wall with her blood.

"Why cut her ass, which, due to a minute loss of blood must have happened post-mortem. Do you think it was an afterthought?"

"I doubt it Jake. I think everything he does is with a purpose. Notice how he staged the crime scene so that she would be found face down. He is denigrating her beauty and showing the rest of us, once again, that he is in charge. There are marks on her body where some type of tape was used to hold her but that was probably removed ex post facto. As you know many serial killers like to take trophies from the scene."

"What's with the broken glass and photos?"

"Besides the obvious need for a painting surface it also shows his anger toward what he perceives as a happy family. My guess is that the killer comes from a broken home and is a victim of sexual abuse. He is manifesting his anger towards his family on those he is attacking."

"Please don't tell me we should feel sympathetic toward this sick son of a bitch."

"I'm not trying to tell you anything, Jake," said Reed, as they walked into the family's living room. Just trying to draw a profile to help us find him." Both of their eyes were drawn to the wall where The Painter's third message filled the surface:

> When thorough force can negate mishaps derision
> better to have left her in receipt
> hopes enliven work ?
>
> check for malice taken
> attack risking louder scale rhetoric

Walt Wizkowski was standing in front of the wall while ERT personnel were all over the room probing, dusting, measuring and photographing.

"Yet another challenge, eh, Wiz?"

"Notice this is a little different, Reed. First, it's longer, secondly it's divided into two parts, and thirdly he included a question mark. A question mark in a place where there is no need for one. There is definitely something we're missing."

"Stay with it Walt, you'll get it," said Reed as he walked toward Joe Quinn bending over shards of glass, photos and frames on the floor.

"Take a look at this," said Quinn to both Reed and Jake as he pointed to the back of the coffee table. "Notice the scratches all along the side of this but none on any other surface. I've got an idea that there was a scuffle here and Deanna did not go quietly. Perhaps she tripped or pushed the unsub and he fell into or over the coffee table."

"What's your point?" asked Jake

"Simply this, you remember Locard's motto developed back in 1920 that we were taught at the Academy: 'Every contact leaves a trace.' That's the way it is with so many killers. They plan precisely and are so very careful in executing their plans but eventually they make a mistake and get caught. Just like Son of Sam and his well-documented parking ticket. Well, this bastard has left nothing before this. Maybe this time he screwed up."

"Let's hope so Joe, like McDonald's says 'We deserve a break today.'"

~ 28 ~

Generally a dozen people comprise an Evidence Response Team but with the heightening sense of severity there were nearly twice that many dissecting every nook and cranny of the Porter home. Reed watched as one of them turned the family dog over, its throat cut, and carefully bagged it just as they would Deanna. Reed's thoughts momentarily turned to Barney, the lab Jake had given to Scott. It's funny, he mused, here we have vibrant young people being killed in the prime of their lives and I still get repulsed at someone harming an innocent pet.

Joe Quinn walked in and offered Reed a scenario, "It appears that she must've come in through the mud room. He may have been already inside waiting for her and after gaining the upper hand she was taken through the kitchen, into the living room where she was stripped, bound, gagged and mutilated. Her clothes were thrown into a corner and like the others, she was killed with what appears to be a knife. Rather than sever her carotid arteries like he did the first girl this time he punctured her femoral artery and let her bleed out that way."

"Or," added Reed, "he came later, sweet talked his way into the house and then over-powered her. We will know better when the ME tells us the time of death. Where are the parents?"

"The girl's father, Wayne Porter, was away on a business trip. He found the body when he returned late last night. His wife died several years ago from cancer. He said that he spoke with Deanna earlier in the day but when he called later there was no answer. He suspected that her cell phone would be in her purse and a quick look confirmed that. It has been taken to the lab to examine. Perhaps the killer contracted her earlier."

"I doubt that. He is too careful. Besides he's a stalker. I'm sure he was watching her and knew when was the best time to act. It's not coincidental that the father was out of town."

Jake was talking to Wayne Porter who was sitting at the kitchen table, his head in his hands. His eyes, droopy naturally, were more so from his having had no sleep, and were bloodshot from the tears that came easily.

"Mr. Porter," asked Jake. "Do you know how the killer could have gotten into your house?"

"Please, call me Wayne. I would guess it wasn't locked Detective. I always told Deanna to be sure and lock it but she felt it wasn't important because, you know, we live in Maine."

"Is there anyone who would want to hurt your daughter?"

"I can't imagine who. I didn't care for the boy she was seeing for the past few months, Brandon Hancock. He dropped out of school and was working on cars out at Casey's in South Windham. I've heard it said that he smoked marijuana and I had to speak to him about getting my daughter home on time but I don't believe he would do this."

"You said, *was seeing?*"

"Yea, they broke up about a week ago. Can't say I was sorry."

"Do you know why, Mr., er...Wayne?"

"Not really. Deanna was upset about it but only said they had an argument and were going to see other people. She is almost 19 and a good girl. I really didn't get too involved in her dating. I never had to. Do you know how hard it is to raise a teenage girl by yourself, Detective?" If only Cathy was alive, maybe Deanna still would be" With that he covered his eyes with his hands and sobbed uncontrollably.

Jake put his hand on Wayne Porter's shoulder and gave it a reassuring squeeze but said nothing before walking out.

Steve Mangino, dusting for prints, looked up after over-hearing the conversation and said as much to himself as anyone, "It's understandable that he's devastated. Imagine losing your wife and then your daughter at the age of nineteen." As Reed walked away from the rhetorical musing Mangino glanced at him and realized what he had said.

"Hey Reed, Christ. I'm sorry... I wasn't thinking...."

"It's alright, Steve. Just get me something that will help catch this bastard."

~ 29 ~

Lieutenant John Bradbury had seen nothing like it in the 27 years he had served in the Maine State Police. Long and lean with dark features and a thin face and neck marked by a lengthy scar earned years ago trying to break up a barroom brawl, he had climbed through the ranks the old-fashioned way, and since he was eighteen months away from retirement he figured that he "didn't need this shit."

Maine hadn't had a serial killer since John Joubert in 1982 and that didn't really count, he reasoned, since he had only killed once in Maine before moving to Nebraska to continue his rampage.

He stepped into the Troop B barracks in Gray with the intent of finding out just what progress was being made in "The Painter" case. He was well aware that shit ran downhill and nowhere quicker than in law enforcement.

As a Lieutenant he served under a Major of Operations and had two Sergeants under him in Southern CID 1. Reed and he had worked together for more years and on more tough cases than he would care to admit. He had no interest in micro-managing him and had it not been for the quickly escalating, high profile of this case he would not be involved.

Once again, for what had recently seemed never-ending, the detectives were seated around the long tables that took up much of the conference room. When Bradbury walked into the room a hush of respect emerged.

"Morning, men," he began. "Don't let me interfere with your meeting. I'm just here to sit in and get brought up to speed. Reed, where are we?"

"This one has got us working night and day, Lieutenant," said Reed, who was standing in front of the dry erase board with a large map of greater Portland depicted. "The first vic was found here in Gorham," he continued, making a dot with an orange hi-lighter. "The second girl was killed here in Brunswick and now the third here in Windham." He connected the three dots by making a triangle.

Jake Lewis spoke up, "All three murders were committed within 30 minutes of where we're located. Generally, serial killers commit crimes in an area they're familiar with - their 'comfort zone' - and often, for safety sake, exit routes etcetera, the first is the closest to their home. As they get more confident they may branch out some."

Bradbury asked, "What about the victimology - do we have a pattern?"

"Two blondes and a brunette - all students. One in high school, two in college, ages 19-23. One comes from Reading, Mass. one from Portsmouth, New Hampshire and one from Windham, Maine. All killed by a knife, a note with a cryptic code left at each scene which we haven't solved yet. Two painted on the scene with the blood of the victim, the other brought to the scene. In each case there has been a body part removed; a breast, a hand, a portion of her buttocks. The first was killed in an apartment on a Thursday, the second outside on a Saturday and the third in her home on a Monday."

"Are we sure these are not random attacks," asked Frank Durgin. "Could he be out cruising the streets, sees someone who triggers a reaction and then attacks?"

"Highly unlikely Frank," responded Reed, pouring himself a glass of water from the Poland Spring dispenser. "Notice the lack of evidence at each crime scene; no footprints, no finger prints, no signs of forced entry, no witnesses. This unsub wears gloves, has stalked his victims establishing an understanding of their habits, and is what is characterized as an 'organized' killer."

"What else do we know about him?" asked Tom Lombardo.

"Judging from my previous experience he will be a white male between twenty-five and thirty-five years of age. We know that he dehumanizes his victims and probably hates all women. He is insecure yet intelligent. He probably appears non-threatening which has allowed him to get into two girls residences and is probably well-spoken."

"Regular Joe - the guy next door," said Durgin.

"Oh, and one more thing," Reed added. "Since he has killed

three girls in the last ten days he must have a job that allows him to travel without arousing suspicion. Possibly a salesman of some type."

"Reed, is there anything that we need to do that hasn't been done?" asked Bradbury.

"We have everyone possible working on this case, John. We have cancelled all vacations until this bastard is caught and most of the guys haven't had a day off since he began. All of the surrounding forces have increased their visibility and we have been in contact with the heads of security at each of the colleges in Maine since he appears to be concentrating on students."

"What about the high schools - that must be a problem, especially now that the third victim is a high school student."

"The problem we have is a public relations issue because the television stations are clamoring for information and obviously much of greater Portland is gripped with fear."

"Do we want to turn this over to the PIO," asked Bradbury, referring to the Public Information Officer that is employed by the State Police.

"If you don't mind, John, I'd rather have all media statements made by me. This has the potential to be a nightmare if we're not careful."

Jake stood, as much to stretch as to be heard, "Naturally we've held back some information from the public including the graphic actions perpetrated on the bodies and the content of the notes, but is it time to release one of those messages or some bit of information in the hope that someone out there might step up because they suspect something? The media is already calling this wacko 'The Painter' based on his choice of medium so someone leaked the fact that he has been using the girls' blood to leave notes."

Reed responded, "That's why I'd like all of the information to be disseminated by me. I'd ask that none of you respond to any of the microphones or tape recorders you're going to have stuck in your face. I want Wiz to have a little more time to work on the messages, Jake, before we turn it over to Quantico or release bits of it to the public. Let me handle the shit storm and try to diffuse it to the best of my ability. Lord knows we won't have any students in school if this continues."

~ 30 ~

The meeting continued for another twenty minutes as the group went over individual assignments, coordination with local police departments, and the handling of press conferences, when Walt Wizkowski, holding a cell phone against his ear, announced, "We may have a break. The lab has identified blood at the scene of the Windham case to be different from the vic."

"Did the sonofabitch actually leave a clue?" asked Joe Quinn.

"Remember how we surmised that Deanna may have knocked the unsub over a coffee table. Well, the ERTs found shards of glass with blood stains under a chair. He may have missed those when cleaning up his scene. They just determined that the blood on that glass - the blood that belongs to the killer - is AB negative"

"Is that significant?" asked Frank Durgin.

"It sure could be," the Wiz replied with a note of excitement in his voice. "It's one of the rarest blood types there is. Only one person in a hundred has AB negative. This doesn't guarantee anything, and it doesn't make it easier to catch him but it certainly narrows the playing field if we are lucky enough to get similar evidence in the future."

"Yea," piped up Quinn in response to Wizkowski's enthusiasm, "we just need to catch him and make sure he's bleeding so we'll know if we've been successful."

"Oh, trust me," said Joe Lombardo, "if I catch him he'll be bleeding. In fact, having his DNA taken will be the least of his problems."

~ 31 ~

After the departmental meeting Reed followed up on a couple of loose ends surrounding the death of Deanna Porter. He had learned that she had come promptly home after cheering practice with only a quick stop at Patches. A check with an employee, who remembered seeing her shortly after 7:00 p.m., verified this.

Tom Lombardi had been given the task of speaking with Brandon Hancock and it wasn't long before he called to speak with Reed. "Yea, I found him out working at Casey's," Tom began, "and Reed, he's an arrogant prick who I don't like even a little."

"You don't have to like him Tom," Reed responded, "just question him. What did he say about Deanna?"

"He said that she had it coming to her. His exact words were, 'It serves the little cock-tease right. She must've pissed somebody else off.' Can you imagine saying that about someone who was just murdered?"

"Where was he at the time Deanna was killed?"

"That's just it, he says he doesn't know. He remembers playing pool at The Nice Rack off 302 and then went home to watch a movie. He admits to smoking a joint and then says he went to bed but there is no one to verify his alibi. He lives by himself."

"Have you followed up with people at The Rack?"

"Not yet. I'm headed there next."

"The ME has placed Deanna's death between 6:00p.m and 10:00p.m. and since we know cheering practice got over at 7:00 and the clerk saw her soon after we know it must have been between 7:30 and 10:00 that she was killed. Let me know what you find."

"Will do."

Reed scheduled a press conference for 3:00 at the Gray barracks and although it was only a bit after 2:00 p.m. reporters, photographers, columnists and even citizens with no affiliation to the media, but were simply scared or fascinated, had begun to file into the conference room.

While he never cherished the idea of going in front of a sea of microphones, Reed recognized the need to try and allay the fear of the masses. That was always the tight rope that law enforcement officials were forced to walk. They tried to hold back as much information as possible so only the guilty person would know the particulars and so as to not petrify the populace, yet they needed to release some information in the chance that some family member or neighbor might have the sense that something is wrong and notify the police.

"Susan," Reed asked, "are the cameras all set in the conference room?"

"They're all set," she replied. "Do you really think the killer will attend the press conference?"

"I have no idea but we have to be ready in case. It wouldn't be the first time that a serial killer tried to get close to the case to see what the police know. We know this guy likes to play games and feels he's smarter than we are so he would probably take great pleasure in coming in disguise. I have notified all of the detectives to be alert for anything that doesn't look just right in terms of clothing, make-up, hair, etcetera."

"Can we charge admission for this today," asked Susan in jest. "It would pay for the annual picnic."

"Hell," piped up Cassie watching the cars starting to line up along Route 236, "the parking concession might do that."

By the time it was 3:00 the detectives had moved a dozen more chairs into the conference room and there was a standing room crowd. Reed stepped to the podium and stared out at the gathering. The lights of television cameras were turned on and for a minute he understood what it must be like to be Tom Cruise at the premiere showing of a movie. He thought of Deanna and snapped back.

"I'd like to thank you," he began, pushing against the podium with both hands, "for being here today and hope that we can be of mutual assistance to one another. As you are no doubt aware, a 19 year old girl, Deanna Porter, was killed in Windham two days ago.We have every reason to believe that this is the third person killed by the same person, a psychopathic serial killer you in the media have begun calling, 'The Painter.'

It is true that at each of the crime scenes there was a message left that was painted in blood. Thus far we have been unable to decipher what the messages mean but we know the killer is taunting us and probably believes he is superior intellectually to us.

In each murder a knife was used but there have been virtually no clues left at the crime scenes. The killer is what is known as an organized killer in that he is careful, deliberate and comes prepared with a weapon, removing it when he is done. We believe that his actions are premeditated and he has been stalking his victims prior to the act which has led to no witnesses. As to victimology, all three were attractive young ladies and students.

Beyond that, and the use of a knife, there is little that is similar. Each lived in a different state but were murdered within 30 minutes of here. If I may speak to what is generally known about serial killers it may provide a base of understanding for who or what we are looking for.

In the State of Maine we have never had a true serial killer, one who has no predetermined number of victims nor any set frequency of activity. We have had spree killings where several people were killed at once, or shortly thereafter, but the two are very different.

First, the serial killer is most likely guilty of what is called the 'homicidal triad.' This means he has probably demonstrated at least two of the following: bed-wetting at an inappropriate age, a pleasure in starting fires, and has displayed cruelty to small animals or children.

The man we are looking for probably possesses these characteristics: low self-esteem, a need for power, intelligence, hates his father and mother because he has been sexually abused, has an inability to have intimate relationships, has demonstrated deviant sexual behavior and will abuse either drugs or alcohol. Sadly, the FBI believes there are 5,000 people killed each year by serial killers most of whom are never captured."

Reed went on to discuss most of the same topics that he had spoken to the department about earlier and then made a general plea to the public: We would ask that if any of you have information that you feel may be pertinent to this case please contact the Maine State Police. If you feel that someone you know is acting strangely then do not confront this person but rather, get in touch with us. Much of what you can do to protect yourself is common sense but must be followed. Be sure to keep your doors and windows locked, let loved ones know where you are at all times and do not go anywhere alone if you can help it."

Reed provided contact numbers and a bit more information and then he opened it up to questions. There were several of these by writers and news reporters relative to the case but it was the last question, posed by a young lady with no media affiliation, that most affected him and would be heard most often as a sound bite the next day on the radio and television news shows.

"Sergeant Sanderson," she began, "I am single, live alone and neither own, nor know how to use, a weapon. Is there any reason why I should not be scared to death when I go to bed tonight?"

~ 32 ~

The late fall winds whipped the multi-colored leaves across the grass long dormant. Small spirals formed mini-tornadoes as the bare trees bowed under the pressure. Men and women wrapped their dark coats around themselves as much to protect them from the bitter cold as to demonstrate the stark solemnness of the occasion.

Reed walked slowly among the grave stones in Evergreen Cemetery. The body of Deanna Porter was being lowered into her final resting place. In her honor Windham High School had cancelled classes and the students, along with most of the townspeople, had turned out en masse to pay their last respects.

In several locations around the cemetery plain clothes detectives conversed with cordless microphones while cameras inconspicuously shot footage of all in attendance in the hope that the perpetrator might appear to offer a final good bye.

Reed was standing beside a giant blue spruce some eighty feet above the ceremony when he noticed a man with leather jacket, jeans and motorcycle boots appear to the right of the assemblage. His long hair hung below a dark blue ski cap onto his shoulders, his hands jammed into his front pockets. The man proceeded to a distance of about fifty feet from the grave site where he leaned against an oak and moved his head furtively as if to determine the identity of those in attendance.

"Do you see him on your left?" came Jake's voice in Reed's ear.

"I do. Do you recognize him?"

"No, but it sure seems that he doesn't fit in and doesn't want to be recognized either. Should we pick him up?"

"Let's wait a couple of minutes and see."

The stranger removed a cigarette pack from his coat pocket and lit one with a lighter, blowing a smoke circle into the afternoon wind.

As the graveside service was coming to a close and the casket had been lowered into the ground many students stepped closer to throw maroon and white flowers, Windham's colors, into the grave site before dispersing. Most hugged or held someone beside them and the sounds of crying filled the air as they walked toward their vehicles.

Only Wayne Porter, a pair of funeral home employees in black suits, and a couple of others remained when Reed saw the stranger begin walking toward the grave.

Immediately … "he's moving," crackled in Reed's ear.

Jake circled to the right putting the stranger between he and Reed. He then walked cautiously toward the grave.

Wayne Porter, sensing the movement, glanced toward the motion and looked up. It was then that a look of recognition crossed his face. "Hello, Brandon."

"Hello, Mr. Porter. If you don't mind I'd like to say good bye to Deanna." He didn't wait for an answer but instead reached into his right front jean pocket, removed an object and threw it into the grave.

Whatever it was had barely landed on the flowers when Jake Lewis had the man in a full-nelson headlock. Reed stepped forward and asked Porter if he knew the man. "Oh yes," was the reply. "That's Brandon Hancock."

"And what did he throw into the grave?"

"I don't know," responded Porter.

The two of them walked around to the middle of the grave and looked down. There on top of the flowers was a used condom filled with a milky liquid.

"You sick bastard, Brandon. No wonder she didn't want to go out with you," said Porter turning away from the grave. "How dare you come here and desecrate her memory."

"Fuck You! I thought I'd give her a gift she could take with her for eternity – something to remember me by."

Reed grabbed the young man by the arm and walked him to his Impala.

~ 33 ~

Jake left the funeral with a foul taste in his mouth and as he left the cemetery he remembered that he had promised his sister that he would stop in to see her son who was playing a youth league football game. His nephew, Nathan, had often listened to Jake talk about his high school football exploits and had developed a bond with the older man. At family holidays Jake made a point to throw a foot ball with the boy and he knew that it would mean a lot if he went to a couple of his games.

As Jake headed down Blackstrap Road heading for Falmouth he came to the intersection of Route 100 and came to a stop behind a station wagon with a young boy in the back making faces at him. Jake waved at the boy and as he waited for a response he looked beyond and noticed a black Cadillac Escalade traveling south in front of him. He looked quickly and recognized a small decal in the right corner of the rear window and noticed that it did have a Maine license plate but was not able to discern the letters or numbers on either.

Unable to move due to both the car in front of him and a steady stream of traffic turning on to Blackstrap, he watched as the vehicle drove away before deciding to turn on his lights. The woman driving the station wagon in front of him could not pull into the traffic crossing in front of her, was not sure if the lights were being directed toward her, and was not sure what she should do, so she put the car in park. Several seconds later Jake backed up, went around her, and merged onto Route 100. With his lights flashing he sped down the road forcing cars to pull to the shoulder and it took less than a minute for him to come up behind the black SUV which had pulled over to let him pass. After Jake had put his cruiser in park and was walking slowly toward the driver side door with his hand on his pistol he glanced at the decal in the rear window. He read the message 2QT2BSTR8 and noticed the small rainbow on the other side before he got to the driver's door.

Inside were two young ladies in the front seats with short haircuts and worried looks. The woman sitting behind the wheel spoke first. "Did I do something wrong officer?"

Jake, realizing that this obviously was not the vehicle he was looking for, thought about giving her a lecture about driving too fast and then letting her off with a warning but then decided that there was no reason to lie. "No, ma'am. We are looking for a similar make automobile but I realize now that this is not the one. I'm sorry to have disturbed you. Keep driving safely and have a great day."

"Thank you, officer. You do the same. And good luck with your search."

~ 34 ~

The Painter slipped a pair of thin plastic gloves on over his hands making sure they were taut and comfortable. He then picked up a piece of 11x14 white construction paper and turned it in a manner just so. It was not easy writing while lying on his mattress but he had had practice.

Beside him was a yellow-lined piece of paper with a series of words arranged in three lines. He read and re-read the words being sure that he could both understand and duplicate. It was to be the next message to the police and, as always, he would be concise and careful not to make any mistakes or blemishes. He took his job seriously.

He glanced at the blood in the vial that he had earlier taken from Deanna Porter and softly swirled it in small circles. *The essence of life,* he thought. More importantly, it came in handy in the creation of this note. Besides, he figured that she wouldn't mind – she didn't need it anymore.

He poured the blood into a plastic cup and then picked up the small plastic bristled brush that had been left for him beside his television. He was deliberate in his attention to detail and, as in each instance before, his work passed his inspection. More importantly he was sure 'The Voice' would be happy with his work.

> Dread can come many times
> before others pray
> cancel every case

He used up all of the blood that he had in the vial - all that was left of Deanna Porter. His planning had been precise and it had allowed him to complete the message with virtually none left over. He thought ahead to what might be needed for the next time, the next message, but then realized that he didn't need to worry.

That was the beauty of his work – there was a seemingly endless supply of paint.

~ 35 ~

Reed sat facing Brandon Hancock in a gray folding chair in his office at the barracks in Gray and asked the toughest question first. "Why did you kill Deanna Porter?"

Hancock's eyes blazed hatred as he replied. "I didn't kill her. I hated her for teasing me and then dropping me but I didn't - I wouldn't, kill her."

"What was that scene at the grave all about today?"

"I can't stand him either. She told me that her father didn't want her to go out with me. I wasn't good enough for his precious little 'Dee Dee.' Fuck him."

"Brandon, there is any number of young girls at the high school or older who would go out with you - and probably any number in this day and age who would sleep with you. Why the big fascination with Deanna?"

"Don't you get it? For me she was a step up the ladder. Most 'good' girls don't want to go out with me. Getting laid isn't that hard, but to be dating a popular girl - a trophy girl - that's special."

"I get it."

Hancock continued. "My father left home when I was ten and my old lady had so many guys coming and going that I couldn't keep track. One of them beat me up one night for not obeying him. Fuck him. I lied about my age to get a job at Casey's, moved out of the apartment we was livin' in and rented a trailer. I been on my own ever since. I'm tired of people telling me I'm not good enough for them but Deanna wasn't like that. We did things together … went to the beach… and the movies."

"So, why did you hate her?"

"After going together all that time I pushed a little, you know, a man's got needs. She used her hand or would blow me but I got tired of that. Finally, one night I had a couple of beers and decided it was time. I got her clothes off'n her but she wouldn't let me go any further. She was crying and I told her to get the hell outa' my trailer. She left and didn't come back. I tried apologizing but she said she couldn't trust me anymore. So, fuck her … she turned out to be like the rest of 'em"

"Do you know anyone who would hate her enough to kill her?" asked Reed

"Not unless she was holding out on some other dude. Like I said before - if she was doing that, then she had it coming."

"You're wrong Brandon. No one deserves that type of death - not even you!"

~ 36 ~

The sun had long since set when Reed decided it was time to go home. Taking a right at the Dry Mills store for the trip back to Raymond he turned on the car radio and was rewarded with "Running on Empty" by Jackson Browne. How fitting, he thought, as he drove through the silent Maine night, the wet snow providing a white canvas on which to drive.

As it often did when away from his job, his mind turned to Amy. He hadn't spoken to her in several days and although she understood how busy he was, he castigated himself for not having called sooner. He pressed 2 on the speed dial of his cell phone, the "1" being reserved for voice messages.

"Hello, Reed. How are you holding up?" she answered.

"Hi Babe," he responded. "I'm beat. These 16-18 hour days add up and ..."

"Where are you?"

"I'm just leaving the barracks and heading home. Why?"

"I don't know. I was just thinking about you. I know how hard you work and know this case must be eating you up."

"Oh, it's a bitch all right. We are virtually working around the clock but we haven't made much progress."

"Do you want to stop over for a drink?"

"What'd you say?"

"I asked if you'd like to stop and have a drink. We haven't talked for awhile and we can catch up while you relax for a few minutes."

"I'd like that Aim - it'll take me about fifteen minutes to get there. Do you need anything?"

"All set - don't use your siren. I'll be here."

Amy had taken a small two-bedroom apartment in Naples after she had moved out. It afforded her some space yet was close enough to her job in New Gloucester and to Reed's house in Raymond should Scott need anything.

Reed walked up her driveway to her side door and felt like a high school junior picking up a prom date. He had helped Amy move some things into her apartment but hadn't been there since. He wasn't sure how to act.

"Hi," she said simply as he stepped into the kitchen.

"Hi," he said as he bent to give her a kiss on the forehead. Instead she put her arms around him and gave him a hug, the urgency of which surprised him. "Are you okay?" he asked, softly placing one hand behind her head and pulling her into him.

"Oh Reed. I don't know what I'm doing. I'm afraid - afraid for Scotty, afraid for you - afraid in general. I'm just so confused by all that's going on inside me and I don't know what to think. I keep thinking, hoping, that tomorrow will be better but I wake up as confused as I was the day before."

Reed basked in the fragrance of her hair that he knew so well and held her close. He started to say something but was caught off guard as she turned away, took him by the hand and led him to her bedroom where she pulled him down on top of her.

His mouth met hers in an exigency of tongues melding in moist competition, their hands were like snake tongues, seizing, grabbing, grasping. Her fingers reached beneath his shirt and then beneath the belt of his trousers squeezing the roundness of his ass.

He felt her chest heaving and rolled beside her, his hand clumsily unbuttoning the buttons on her blouse. Their mouths remained fused as she unfastened his belt and reached inside. Holding her bra aside he took her nipple between his teeth while in a manner equally as rough she stroked the length of his hardness.

Without removing his mouth he slid his pants down over his ankles. Amy arched up, put a hand on each side of her pants and pushed. Again their mouths met in a symphony of passion. She kicked off her pants and underwear and then pulled him on top of her once again,

Reed, who intended to show her how much he loved her, attempted to enter her slowly but she would have none of it. She wrapped her legs around him and locked her heels against the back of his thighs. Patiently at first he tried to establish a gentle rhythm but moments later his piston-like motion, carved from the lust of separation was matched by her movements and primordial screams. "Oh, oh, oh, Reed ... don't stop... it's been so long."

Together they roiled as one, their bodies united in primal passion until Amy felt a cascade of pleasure engulf her. But still Reed did not stop. Instead, he seized her hips in his hands, his thrusts becoming longer and more primitive until once again she felt a wave of euphoria sweep over her and then a shudder as he climaxed and collapsed onto her shoulder.

After they had readjusted their positions she ran her hands down the back of his head feeling the perspiration in his hair and then lower onto the middle of his back pulling him close. Moments later Reed rolled off of her onto his back

"Amy, I don't know what to say."

She placed her head on his shoulder and draped her arm across his chest. "Then don't say anything," she replied, kissing him gently on the cheek.

They fell asleep in each other's arms.

~ 37 ~

Winter is often an early visitor to Maine and most often wears out its welcome. Harsh winters make for good neighbors and most people lock neither their home nor their car and, although the spate of murders altered many people's thinking, old habits are hard to break.

This is a handy bit of knowledge to possess if your intent is to kill.

Randy Kingston was engaged in quiet conversation in The Chalet on the campus of Saint Joseph's College in Standish. Originally designed with a ski motif forty years earlier, when it was an all-girls school, The Chalet had undergone several interior design renovations but still served beer to those of legal age and offered students a place to study quietly or meet socially.

Because it was a Monday night it was inordinately quiet but he didn't need a full house to enjoy himself, just conversation with the right young lady. On this occasion he had found just such an individual and he was pleased with himself for having asked Anne Shea if she wanted to come back to his dorm room to study.

Anne was a cute little brunette whose hair was straight and everything else was curvy. She had eyes that glistened and hands that danced when she spoke manifesting itself in an upbeat personality. The word around campus was that she was "easy" but Randy couldn't care less – she was friendly and she was coming to his room. Life was good.

Although he was not taking a course in Anatomy and Physiology he was more than willing to study it. As a sophomore he was a year ahead of Anne but because he was diffident around girls he "scored" much less than his friends. This had bothered him through high school in Rutland, Vermont but not so much that he could change his personality or dating style. It was considered a curse if girls just wanted to be your "friend" and yet he had never found the secret to eliminating this annoyance. He had been taught to appreciate women and treat them with respect. It was his parents fault he figured.

Anne told him that she wanted to go back to her dorm for a couple of minutes which was fine with him because it would allow him time to pick up a bit before she arrived. He placed a bill on the counter and headed out the back door pulling up his ski sweater to shield himself from the typical biting wind coming off Sebago Lake.

He remembered that he had backed in and headed for his black PT Cruiser. There was a light dusting of snow on his vehicle so he brushed off the driver's side window and climbed into the front seat. As he reached to put his key in the ignition he sensed movement behind him and the last vision Randy had was that of a man in his rearview mirror. His eyes registered more surprise than fear but he never felt the cold steel of the hunting knife that sliced across his throat. He saw the splatter on the steering wheel and dashboard before he heard the gurgling sound. He reached into the warm wetness at his neck then softly slipped into a silent abyss.

As always there was more work to be done before the killer could return home. It was done with precision and panache. He headed for home with the warm glow of satisfaction radiating through his being. Excellence, he realized, in any endeavor, provides pleasure.

~ 38~

It had been a quiet night and Jesse Hastings decided that it wouldn't hurt if she closed The Chalet an hour early. Normally she would stay open until 11:00 on weeknights and midnight on the weekends, but as manager she had some discretion in this.

After announcing "Last Call" to the half-dozen students who were still sitting in the wooden booths she went about picking up and mopping up her bar and the equipment that accompanied.

She was putting chairs up on the few tables so she could sweep when the phone rang.

"Chalet," she said succinctly.

"Hi. This is Anne Shea. I was there about twenty minutes ago."

"Yea, Hi Anne. I know who you are. What's up?"

"Well, I was supposed to meet Randy Kingston here in his room and according to his roommate he has not been back. He's not still there is he?"

"No. He left just after you did … a few minutes ago. I saw him go out the back door."

"His roommate says he drives a black four-door PT Cruiser with Vermont plates. Could you look to see if it's still there. I'd appreciate it."

"Sure, Anne … just a minute."

Jesse threw her wet rag onto the counter and walked out the back door into the small parking lot. There were about a dozen cars parked against the periphery of the woods and it didn't take her long to spot the Cruiser.

She walked over to it and tried to see in but between a light snow layer and a driver's side window that appeared to be fogged, she could not determine if there was anyone inside. She received no response from saying "Randy… Randy," so she reached for the door handle.

A gasp escaped her lips as she found Randy's body slumped back against the driver's seat that had been adjusted to lean almost into the back seat.

In the moonlight of the Maine winter she saw Randy Kingston, his throat slashed, his left eye removed and a rolled up piece of paper inserted in the socket where it had been.

She fell to the pavement, her scream piercing the sanctity of the night.

~ 39 ~

Reed finished popping a double batch of Orville Redenbacher's gourmet popcorn – Butter Lovers, thank you – and had mixed a can of lemonade in a two-quart plastic pitcher. Sandy was sitting in his customary oak rocker while Scott was on the floor next to Barney when he walked in. A roaring fire blazed in the fireplace offering crackling sounds as well as warmth to the cozy room.

This had become a Monday night ritual at their home even as busy as he had been, as all three of the Sanderson males would settle around the television to watch Charlie Sheen in the comedy "Two and a Half Men." Reed, like the rest of civilized society, recognized that the show was politically incorrect but farcically humorous nonetheless.

Of course there were the obvious familial comparisons to the characters depicted and it gave Sandy great enjoyment to poke fun at Scott comparing him to Jake, the pudgy boy on the show played by Angus Jones who was going through puberty.

"Ya' know, Scotty, the yearly swimsuit issue of Sports Illustrated will be here soon and you know you won't be able to see that one."

"At least until Sandy sees it, added Reed."

"Will they have 80 year olds in this year's edition, Sandy? asked Scott.

"I hope not but I don't want you getting any ideas."

"But Sandy, I only want to see the magazine to read the articles … you know, the quality writing."

"It's Playboy Magazine that you save that speech for Scott, when your mom's around."

"I am thinking about becoming a doctor and feel learning about the female anatomy might get me jump-started."

"I've heard this all before Scott," said Sandy, his eyes twinkling. "Years ago your dad couldn't wait for National Geographic to come out so he could see the topless women in those African tribes. He tried to convince me that he wanted to be an anthropologist."

Reed just rolled his eyes at the good-natured bantering. He missed these opportunities to see his son joust with his father when his work dominated his life.

Shortly after the show was over Reed's phone rang – a good sound, a bad sign. It was Jake Lewis on the other end and his voice had the urgency of a three-alarm fire. "Reed, you're not going believe it – there's been another murder... this one's at Saint Joseph's College ... and it's a MALE student."

"Are you sure it's our guy, Jake? Why a male? Could it be a copycat?"

"We don't have lab reports, of course, I just got the word. But there is a note and the throat was cut like the others."

"Where was the body found?"

"In the victim's car in a parking lot behind the campus pub."

Reed by now had changed his pants and thrown on shoes and a jacket. "Who found the body?"

"The manager of the pub – she got a call from a girlfriend or someone."

"Where are you, Jake – I'm out the door."

"About fifteen minutes out. The campus police called the Sheriff's Department and they're on the scene. See ya' soon."

Reed walked over to Scott, kissed him on the top of the head and said, There's been another murder. I've got to run."

"You're really going to meet another woman aren't you Uncle Charlie," Scott replied in an attempt at humor referencing the show they had just watched.

"I wish I was," Reed replied. "No, I don't – you know what I mean... Good night Scott, night Sandy. Barney, you hold the fort."

~ 40 ~

Saint Joseph's College was owned, and in large part run, by the Sisters of Mercy, an order of nuns who traced their lineage to Catherine McAuley of Ireland who espoused "doing ordinary things inordinately well." Unfortunately this did not refer to the killing of a male student on the lakeside campus in Standish.

It did not take Reed long to reach the campus from his home in Raymond and he was one of the first on the scene. The Sheriff's Department had closed off the campus by blocking the front driveway on Whites Bridge Road, for all intents and purposes the only way to enter the campus.

Reed drove up to The Chalet and walked behind to the PT Cruiser as a member of the ERT was removing the note from Randy Kingston's eye socket and placing it in a plastic bag.

"Can you believe he cut the kid's eye out?" he asked Reed.

"At this point I would believe about anything."

It was to be yet another long night for Reed, the detectives of the CID and the rest of the Evidence Response Team. No one in The Chalet or those interviewed on campus had seen anything suspicious. There were seemingly no fingerprints at the scene suggesting that once again the killer had worn gloves. A flat-bed truck had been sent for which would take the Cruiser to Augusta to examine for clues.

After speaking with the victim's roommate and several of his friends there was no information gleaned that pointed to anyone in particular. They would interview everyone whose room was above The Chalet, in what was a first-year female dorm. Reed would leave that up to deputies in the Sheriff's department and several Windham cops since those two organizations shared jurisdiction when it came to the College.

Glenn Boarin, the head of Campus Security, was not on duty when the murder occurred but was quickly summoned and after Reed conferred with him and the duty officers he was no further ahead.

"Years ago, said Boarin, we used to have a little guard shack out front where all visitors had to stop and state their business but it became a public relations nightmare so the College did away with it. Hell, it might have come in handy tonight."

"I'm not so sure Glenn," Reed replied, as he was taking down the officers names. "The man we are looking for is one smart bastard. No one saw anybody suspicious. He may have not even driven on campus."

After that meeting Boarin took Reed to the student life center where he picked up a folder with a red label marked Randall Kingston. Color coded to delineate his graduating class, the folder held all of the academic, social, and civic information pertinent to his time on campus as well as all of the materials from Rutland high school.

His parents, Blake and Kendra Kingston of 114 Iriqois Avenue, had not been notified and he decided that he would leave that up to Jake. After many years on the job that was one aspect of it that he had never developed an immunity to. He knew only too well the sounds of anguish and agony, often re-visiting him in his nightmares.

The ME had now arrived along with a rescue ambulance and what seemed like every law enforcement official in Cumberland County. The tiny Catholic College which was founded in Portland in 1912 and moved to the shores of Sebago Lake in 1956, had not experienced such a scene since a coed had allegedly set fire to a dorm room years earlier.

After several hours of interviewing, examining and commiserating, Reed was preparing to leave when Ray Wilson, a member of the Windham Police Department, saw him and offered a terse overview of the incident. "I just can't understand it, Reed. The sonovabitch was waiting for the kid in the backseat of his own car and then cut his throat. And if that isn't bad enough he cuts his eye out. Christ, it's like we're watching a god damn horror movie."

"Actually, Ray, it's worse than that. It feels like we're *living* a horror movie."

~ 41 ~

The killer had previously done his due diligence and learned there was an old tennis court long since grown over in the woods behind The Chalet. By following that path he was neatly able to disappear into the dense pines and come out behind the baseball field. He had parked on a inclined dirt road beside the field off of Wards Road which bordered the college. As usual, he was neat, clean and inconspicuous, carefully brushing over his tracks with a pine bough, eliminating his footprints in the light snow.

When he reached his vehicle he wiped his knife on a towel, placed Randy Kingston's eye in a baggie that he had brought for just such an occasion, and removed his gloves and gray work overalls that were splattered with blood. Throwing them in a burlap bag he turned the key in the ignition and began the drive home.

As he drove slowly down Whites Bridge Road he looked above at the full harvest moon that hung in the sky like a medallion. He hadn't gone far when he encountered a Sheriff's car screaming toward the campus and then, just before turning onto Route 302, another unmarked car flew past, its interior light flashing. He glanced in the rear view mirror, a smile enveloping his face. *How little they know, how frustrated they must be.*

~ 42 ~

Reed's phone rang waking him from a restless sleep and for a moment he thought about not answering it. He had not gone to bed until almost 4:00 a.m. and as he rubbed the sleep from his eyes he realized that he still had his clothes on, having fallen asleep on the top of his bed. It seemed that every time he had answered it recently there had been bad news.

On the other line was Walt Wizkowski. "Hey, Wiz, What's up?"

"Reed, listen. I think I've finally solved the codes in the messages! It isn't sentences or phrases - it's the Bible Code. I should have thought of this sooner. You just take the EDLS and …"

"Whoa, Wiz, wait a minute. I'm afraid that you lost me already and you've just begun. Listen, I'm headed to the Barracks. How about I get the men together and let you debrief everyone at the same time. It's 7:30 now, can you be there by 8:30?"

"No problem- should we notify the media?"

"Absolutely not. Let's see what we have first. The fact that the killer does not know what we know may prove to be a huge edge. See you in a bit."

This could be phenomenal news, thought Reed. I can't wait to see what the Wiz has dug up.

Reed called John Bradbury while driving towards the Barracks. "Lieutenant, I'm on my way to Gray. Wiz says he thinks he has solved the riddle of the messages and I thought you might want to be there when he explains it to all of us."

"Thanks, Reed. Absolutely. What time do you expect to get going?"

"I told him 8:30. Most of the guys were at St. Joe's 'til pretty late last night. I'll have Callie get in touch with everyone."

When Reed arrived at the Gray barracks Wiz had already set up two white boards in the conference room and there was a buzz throughout the Division he had not heard in some time.

Susan had prepared a large container of coffee and had it set up on a side table in the conference room. Reed looked around and saw Durgin, Lombardo, Quinn, Costello and Wiz bantering among each other about the most recent murder, the fact that the victim was a male, and any number of things related to the case. Only Jake had not yet arrived and he called to say he was running "a couple of minutes late."

While they were waiting for Jake and Lt. Bradbury to arrive Wiz wrote the messages left by the killer on the boards. He turned the second around and moved it a few feet away.

Message left at the scene in Gorham

BEHOLD THE DEATH O' HEATHENS
THINK OF WHEN INDELIBLE LIABILITIES WILT
LOVING CAN BEGIN WHITHER PREPARATIONS
SHROUD BEFORE DESERVING JUST FRUIT DIVINE

Message left at Bowdoin murder scene

WONDERMENT SEIZES EVERYONE
AWAKEN TO THE GLORY BE
THE CHILD HAS SANCTUMS
IRENIC WILL NEVER SEE

Message left at the crime scene in Windham

WHEN THOROUGH FORCE CAN NEGATE MISHAPS DERISION
BETTER TO HAVE LEFT HER IN RECEIPT
HOPES ENLIVEN WORK?

CHECK FOR MALICE TAKEN
ATTACK RISKING LOUDER SCALE RHETORIC

Message left at the scene at Saint Joseph's College

DREAD CAN COME MANY TIMES
BEFORE OTHERS PRAY
CANCEL EVERY CASE

All of the others settled into the chairs around the long tables with Reed nestled to the right of Wiz and the first board. Jake walked in as Reed was adding powdered cream to his coffee. Cassie popped her head in to announce that, "Lt. Bradbury has been held up but to go ahead and start without him."

Walt Wizkowski looked more like an accountant than a detective. He was thin both in body and in face and he had worn glasses since he was ten. With bushy unmanaged eye brows and an elongated nose he looked almost bird-like. A high squeaky voice fit his frame. An advanced understanding of computers, and superior intellect led as much to his nickname as simply an abbreviation of his surname and on more than one occasion he had solved cases by deductive reasoning. His excitement resonated as he stood before his peers.

As many of you know the study of codes, cryptography and cipher texts has long been a passion of mine. The word 'cryptography' evolved from the Greek work *kryptos* which means hidden. The goal of a person utilizing cryptography is not to conceal the fact that there is a message, but rather, to disguise the true meaning of the message.

Thus, the killer has purposely placed messages at the four crime scenes. He has challenged us to decipher the meanings of the messages - playing with us, if you will. In the beginning I took the killer's messages at face value. I examined the words and tried to decipher the meaning of the sentences or phrases.

Each seemed to make some degree of sense though often there was an odd word or thought. Because we are taught to 'try to get into the mind of the killer,' I accepted these messages as verbal challenges. As I said in an earlier meeting, the killer obviously has an advanced vocabulary and I got bogged down in words like: *whither, gambits, shroud, sanctums, irenic, etcetera.* It was only after I gave up on taking the messages at face value that I was able to make any headway."

John Bradbury walked into the room offering apologies for being late. "I'm sorry - a pickup went off the road and I stopped to help. Go ahead, Walt, continue."

"Glad to, Lieutenant. You haven't missed much. I've just tried to give some background on how I arrived at what I feel is the solution. Cryptology is generally divided into separate subsets known as substitution and transposition.

The former reference is to the original message, or plaintext, transposing one letter for another, while in the latter the letters being used are re-arranged. Therefore, in transposition the letters maintain their identity but change position within the text. In substitution the letters maintain their position but have their identity altered. The message, after being encrypted, is called cipher text."

He grabbed a blue marker and began to write as he continued speaking. "For example, in transposition we might have the letters KILL THE MAN placed in three vertical lines like this:

KILL
THE
MAN

By replacing the letters in a top to bottom format the message would appear like this: KTMIHALENL. But, as long as the recipient of the message knew there were three lines, he could easily restructure the letters to complete the message as written above.

"Is that what the killer used, Walt?" asked Frank Durgin.

"No, but I want to give you a little background before I tell you what I have found," answered the Wiz.

"Now, if he wanted to use a substitution cipher he could have simply paired the letters of the alphabet with another and substitute one for the other when creating his code. Thus, if A=M, B=X, C=O and T=F you would spell cat: O-M-F. These can be done in a pattern, or to make it more difficult to decipher, at random. More difficult yet, is the substitution of symbols for letters, much like ancient hieroglyphics."

"Once again, this is not difficult if the recipient is aware of the substitution code. Auguste Kerckhohh von Nieuwenhof, one of the founders of cryptology once wrote that a cryptosystem should be secure even if everything about the system is known except the key. This became known as Kerckhoff's Principal and this, gentlemen, is what I have struggled with for the past few weeks."

Tom Lombardo, one hand twirling his ample mustache, asked, "If the killer is going to leave us clues why not give us the code ... or better yet, just write sentences that we can understand?"

"For the killer that wouldn't be any fun. He is showing us that he is smarter than we are and if we want to catch him we are going to have to be more clever."

"Go on Wiz," encouraged Reed.

"Many of the ancient scholars felt that substitution ciphers couldn't be broken due to the huge number of mathematical possibilities there are. Later they discovered that, because in the use of all languages some letters are more commonly used than others, we can mathematically create a solution. This is called frequency analysis."

"In the English language for example, "e" is the most commonly used letter followed by "t" and then "a." The longer the message the more likely it will follow the normal frequencies and the easier it will be to solve. Because the sentences, as written in the messages, made little or no sense, I decided to try frequency analysis, but after much study I was unable to make any progress. So, as you can see, most of what cryptologists go through is trial and error and it can be very time consuming."

"My problem is that I have an English background and attack cryptological problems by examining their verbal structure, perhaps under-estimating the intellect or sophistication of the un-sub."

"The earliest attempts at cryptanalysis dealt with attempts to solve military secrets such as the Black Chamber of Vienna in the late 1700s, and the now-famous Room 40 in Great Britain during World War II where they placed classical scholars with language experts and crosswords addicts and had terrific success."

"This is great, Wiz, but how does it help us with the bastard killing students?" asked Jake, who had leaned forward in his chair.

"Sorry, Jake. I wanted you to see what I went through to reach a solution. Anyway, after trying these methodologies and having no success I was afraid that I couldn't solve these cipher texts until Friday when I listened to *Hotel California* by the Eagles."

~ 43 ~

"You did what?" asked Reed.

"I was driving home when *Hotel California* came on my radio and it hit me. Do you remember when that first came out and people said that if you played it backwards there was a satanic message. The same was said of *Stairway to Heaven* by Led Zeppelin and others and that got me thinking about hidden messages.

In 1997 Michael Drosnin wrote a book that created consternation everywhere. His book, *The Bible Code*, claimed that the Bible contained hidden messages which can be discovered using equidistant letter sequences. These EDLS's are found by examining any text, selecting a starting letter, and then moving forward by a set number of letters.

Drosnin, when doing his research, discovered that by using EDLSs the Bible contained not only words that make sense but complete sentences that resulted in amazing historical events. He claimed that EDLSs formed sentences referencing the assassinations of John and Robert Kennedy, as well as Thomas Edison next to 'light bulb' and Sir Isaac Newton next to 'gravity.' As you can imagine it caused quite a stir in both the academic and religious communities.

Now while many criticize the work because they say that if you find a large enough text phrases can be commonplace if one varies both the starting letter and the number of jumps."

"Which relates to our killer, how?" asked Jake impatiently.

"Well, I decided to try the EDLSs on the messages and I believe I may have hit upon something." Here Wiz grabbed the blue marker and began to make circles around some of the letters in the first message. "Look what appears when I count seven letters in from the beginning and then jump every seven letters after that. You can see in the first line we would have T…H…E and then K…"

Behold The deatH o heathEns   T...H...E
thinK of when IndelibLe liabiLities wIlt   K...I...L...L...I
loviNg can beGin whitHer prepA rations   N...G...H...A
shroud before deserving just fruit divine

"Christ O Mighty," interrupted Joe Quinn. "The Killing has Begun. It spells, *The killing has begun.*"

~ 44 ~

"You are right, Joe, the message that was painted on the wall at Angela Carrington's apartment was "The killing has begun" if you use every seventh letter starting from the beginning.

At this point Reed spoke up. "Wiz did you try any of the other combinations? Is there any way that this could be a weird coincidence?"

"I tried them all, Reed and that's the only combination that formed words."

"That makes sense, Wiz," said Jake, "but I am going ahead to the next message - the one left at Bowdoin - and I came up with letters .. MZYKYELNRLS … which obviously doesn't make any sense."

"That's what I thought too, Jake, but then after a series of trials and error I decided to use every sixth letter in that message., See what that spells."

Again, Joe Quinn, taking to the task with enthusiasm spoke up. R…E…V…E…N…G…E…

"Revenge is Mine."

By now all of the others had caught up and seen how the use of the equidistant 6 sequence had led to the formulation of sentences.

Wiz asked the question, "Does everyone see what I am convinced is the killer's pattern?" With a nod of agreement and general assent Wiz then pushed away the first white board and reached for the second. Turning it around, the group could see that not only had he written the messages, but he also had encircled letters in both. Beneath the third message, which was divided into two sections, were the letters:

TURN THE OTHER CHEEK and **KATAKIUCHI**.

"Note that there was a question mark after the first group,"

Wiz said.

Reed was the first to speak. "Wiz, I can certainly understand the first message but I have no idea what Katakiuchi means. Are you sure that isn't a mistake or a different EDLS?"

"That's what I thought at first, Reed, but because I believed in the pattern, I examined the meaning of the word Katakiuchi on the internet. According to wikipedia it means 'revenge killing' and states that in Japan's feudal past the Samurai class upheld the honor of their family through this practice."

"So, whoever is doing the killing feels that they are acting out of a sense of revenge," John Bradbury offered.

"The last message," Wiz continued, "is the shortest of them all and certainly seems to concur with what Lieutenant Bradbury suggests."

AN EYE FOR AN EYE

Tom Lombardo, who had been slouching, but now sat up in his chair, said, "I notice Wiz, that in each of the notes the EDLS has changed. It went from seven to six to five and in the last note every fourth letter. Why would the killer change the pattern?"

"I'm not really sure, Guy," he replied, "but you are correct, that is definitely the pattern. I tried all of the other sequences and came up with nothing."

Reed rose from his chair and looked out over the conference room before he spoke.

"I'm afraid," he began, "that I have a theory as to why he may have changed the pattern. It's based on the number of the person being killed."

"Number of the person being killed?" repeated Bradbury with a rise in his voice.

"Don't you see, Angela Carrington's note had seven letters in between because she was the seventh - from the end. Carrie Mortenson had six letters in her note and she was 6th from the end... and so on. Our killer," Reed said, pausing to take a deep breath as he looked at the assemblage, "has killed four students - *he intends to kill three more!*"

~ 45 ~

A pall fell over the gathering of law enforcement officials as what Reed had just said sank in. Jake was the first to break the silence. "This crazy bastard intends to kill three more students?" he asked incredulously.

"I believe I'm right, Jake," replied Reed. "Why else would he count down from seven using the letter sequencing method? And why else would he continue to leave clues unless this cat and mouse game is continuing. Notice that he not only feels he's smarter than we are but he also has made attempts to be clever."

"How so, Reed?" asked Bradbury.

"Remember how we found Deanna Porter in her home. Unlike the first two she was positioned with her head in the sofa, her buttocks facing up…"

"And the message was *turn the other cheek*," offered Joe Quinn.

"Right you are, and what was the last message?"

"*An eye for an eye*," answered Quinn.

"And the killer removed the boys eye," said Reed. "So not only is he trying to drive home this point of revenge or retribution, but he is attempting to be clever while doing it."

"Is it that or is the killer purposely taking souvenirs which often occurs?" asked Jake. "Remember, there's been something taken on each occasion. First the breast was removed, then a hand, then a piece of her buttocks and lastly an eye. We all know he's a sick bastard…."

Reed interrupted saying, "Jake, I don't believe he's taking body parts for trophy sake. Whenever that occurs the killer generally takes the same body part again and again. For example, Ed Gein kept skinned-out faces and hung them on the walls of his home while Jerome Brudos kept severed breasts as paperweights. In this case each time it has been different and I believe it is because he is becoming more brazen. I still feel the hand was taken to protect against possible DNA evidence and the breast was possibly an afterthought - a way of showing us his power. The last two, as I stated earlier, may have been just to show us how clever he is."

"Reed, it seems to me that we have a couple of major concerns," began Bradbury. "First, if the killings are revenge driven, as it seems, what is the motivation? Secondly, why would he change his MO and begin killing boys rather than attractive females?"

"I think, Lieutenant, when we find the answer to the first question we'll have the reason for the second. What do these four students – all attending different schools and all coming from different states - have in common, and more importantly, who are the other three kids who have been earmarked to die?"

~ 46 ~

After the departmental meeting the detectives disbanded to do what they do best, or most often; set up interviews, man the phones and carefully analyze the copious notes taken earlier.

Wizkowski, who was given many accolades for his analytical work, was given the task of setting up a later press announcement to disseminate the decoding information. After much discussion it was decided to release the information in the hopes that it would assuage the fears of the general public if it was determined that the killings were not the arbitrary acts of a sadistic serial killer but rather the careful designs of a revenge killer.

"Reed, are you sure you don't want to make the announcement to the press? You've been the point man on all of this," asked Walt.

"I'll be beside you Wiz, for any peripheral questions, but you deserve the credit for all of your hard work. Remember, we won't offer the conjecture of three more killings to come. No sense in creating panic, especially when we don't know the motive. If anyone goes down that path turn it over to me."

"And what will you say, oh wise one?"

"I'll do my best Fred Astaire imitation and try to dance around it like any good politician."

"Maybe Dancing with the Stars would be more timely today Reed."

"Yea, you're right. I've got to modernize my thinking."

Reed spent a few minutes with Jake, Lt. Bradbury and others as they were leaving and then prepared to leave himself when he saw Susan approaching him with a wry expression.

"Charlie Carrington is here to see you," she said. "Do you want me to tell him that you've already gone?"

"Nah, that wouldn't be right. Besides, I've already made plans to be Fred Astaire today I don't see why I can't be David Copperfield also."

"Fred Astaire ... David Copperfield?"

"Never mind Susan, have him come on in."

Reed watched her backside as she departed and was thinking that she often seemed to accentuate her movements for his benefit. His thoughts were interrupted when Charlie Carrington came towards him in his typically energized manner.

"Mr. Carrington, good to see you again."

"I wish I could say the same Sergeant Sanderson. I was in the area on business and thought I'd stop to see what progress, if any, you've made in catching the bastard that killed my daughter."

"Mr. Carrington, as I told you the last time we spoke," Reed began with a conscientious attempt at civility, "we are doing everything in our power to catch your daughter's killer. Virtually every man in our unit is working around the clock. Guys are putting in twenty-hour days, seven days a week and refusing to take either days off or vacation."

"Sergeant, I appreciate your efforts, really I do, I know that you and your men are well-intentioned and I am sure that you have other items on your plate, but I just feel there is more that can be done. As you may have surmised I have a few dollars, as does Wayne and Morty, and we're thinking of hiring a private detective to investigate these murders; not with any desire to usurp any of your authority or denigrate your efforts, but just maybe to provide a fresh look - you know, a new set of eyes."

~ 47 ~

"What did you just say?" asked Reed.

"I said that Wayne and Morty and I are considering hiring a private detective to work on our cases because you have not made the progress that we feel you should have made."

"Who is Morty?"

"Ben Mortenson"

"You know Wayne Porter and Ben Mortenson?" asked Reed with incredulousness.

"Of course I know them. We went to college together and we've remained friendly."

"And you know Blake Kingston?"

"Yes"

"What college did you attend?"

"Bowdoin, replied Carrington. "Class of '87"

"Well, Jesus jumped-up Christ, this might be the relationship rationale behind the killer's motives. Why didn't you tell me that you knew each other? Do you not realize the implication here?"

"Of course we do. That's why we want to hire someone to catch the sonofabitch."

"So, each of you attended Bowdoin College. Were you in the same class?"

"We started together but wound up going separate ways. Blake dropped out when he couldn't afford it, Morty and Wayne transferred out also. We've moved away to different states but have attempted to stay close."

Reed rubbed his chin with his right hand as he often did when perplexed. "Now Mr. Carrington, you are telling me that three of your friends have lost children plus your daughter and you didn't think it was important enough to bring this to our attention. Obviously you pissed somebody off if, as we're being told, the murders are revenge killings."

"Who said anything about revenge killings?"

"Just today one of the detectives broke the code on the messages being left at the crime scenes and all four point to these killings being revenge oriented. If you'll excuse me I am going to set up a meeting for all of the parents, along with our Division. We need to get to the bottom of this and see if there is any other pertinent information that you have not shared with us. This is the biggest break we've had."

~ 48 ~

Jake Lewis lived in a condominium in the Deering section of Portland, just fifteen miles from the Police Headquarters in Gray via the Maine Turnpike. More importantly he was just minutes from downtown Portland and the city's Old Port section where erstwhile singles spend their evenings in search of that elusive "Mr. or Mrs. Right."

Jake had moved in several years ago after his wife of three years had left him for another man and "a life of sanity, where I don't have to worry about you coming home alive." He originally moved into an apartment but, like much of greater Portland, the complex was converted into condominiums and Jake purchased his two bedroom upper unit when given the opportunity.

So, too, did the other inhabitant in the unit below, Mrs. Weinstein, an eighty-three year old grandmother. She told him that she "felt secure" knowing that a police officer lived in the building and while Jake was continually being ribbed for living in a "swinging singles pad" he went out of his way to help Mrs. Weinstein carry in groceries or take the trash that she piled in a red wagon, to the end of the driveway.

Further, he had originally lived in the downstairs unit, but when he saw that an elderly lady was moving in upstairs Jake had offered to switch apartments to make it easier for her. For his efforts he was often presented with molasses cookies, blueberry cake or some other confectionary delight.

On this night Reed was parked in his Explorer in a small parking lot adjacent to Jake's building with a clear view of the stairs that ran up the side of the building to his unit.

Unbeknownst to Jake, Reed had done this on several occasions, especially when his travels had taken him to Portland, ever since Jake had shared his concern about the skinheads and a possible retaliation.

Although Reed was working diligently on the case of "The

Painter," not a day went by that he didn't spend time trying to find the killer of his son.

With a cup of Dunkin Donuts hazelnut coffee in his hand and the Celtics game from the west coast turned down low on his radio, Reed was looking at a full moon shining onto the complex's tennis courts when he noticed a dark SUV pull into the driveway to the complex with its lights out. Reed sat up, shut off the car, extinguished the radio and watched as the vehicle came to a stop in front of Jake's building. Reed could see in the moonlight that it was indeed a Cadillac Escalade but could not distinguish any of the characteristics of the two men who exited the vehicle, one on each side.

Dressed in dark clothing the pair glanced about in all directions before stealthily heading toward Jake's steps. Reed removed the pistol from its holster and punched in the number four on his cell phone speed dial. It rang twice before Jake answered.

"What's up partner?" he responded groggily.

"Jake, I'm outside your condo and there are two men heading up your stairs," he said in a loud whisper.

Reed tried to open his car door quietly but the action alerted the two on the stairs and they began to run down and across to their vehicle.

Reed ran across the parking lot, his gun drawn, as lights came on in Jake's condo. "STOP or I'll shoot," he hollered at the pair as the man heading for the driver's side paused and fired a shot that ricocheted off the pavement and landed in a building behind him. Reed dropped to the ground and fired a round of shots, one of which splintered the rear window of the SUV as it peeled away from the parking lot, down the driveway, and out onto Forest Avenue.

By now Jake was running down the steps dressed in flannel pajamas and t-shirt, pistol in his hand.

"Reed, are you alright?" he asked, as lights from around the complex were coming on and people's faces were pressed against their windows.

"Yea, I'm fine," he replied. "It was our friends in the black Escalade and I believe you're right about them wanting to settle a score with you."

"That doesn't surprise me at all. In fact, I really expected something like this and by the way, what the hell are you doing in my yard?"

"I'll tell you about it later. Let me call this in first in case any of the Portland cops on patrol spot the vehicle. Oh and Jake, I got the license plate number this time."

~ 49 ~

It was three days later when Reed and Jake hustled into the lobby of the Holiday Inn Convention Center in Saco, a suburb of Portland. Although they had taken separate vehicles they had arrived at the same time and were a bit later than they had hoped. A conference room had been reserved for the MSP and all of the detectives who had worked on the case were to attend this special meeting which would include the parents of the four murdered students.

Reed observed a small sign in the lobby that read: MSP - York Room. After getting directions from the desk the two meandered until they found the appropriate sign and entered. Already inside were Charlie and Lisa Carrington, Ben and Sarah Mortenson,Wayne Porter, and all of the detectives. Blake and Kendra Kingston, who were traveling the farthest, had not yet arrived but Reed, who looked at his watch and saw that it was 6:50 p.m., asked each of those in attendance to introduce themselves and then began.

"It is not quite seven but I will get us started and assume that the Kingstons will be here shortly. Thank you for making the trip here tonight. Although it is not equidistant for all of you, we tried to make it a bit closer for those who live the farthest away.

We know you have all suffered a great loss recently and although all of the men you see around you, and others, have worked virtually around the clock, we had made little progress until three days ago.

On that day, Walt Wizkowski; Reed pointed to him with an open hand, solved the riddles of the messages at the crime scenes. Also on that day, Charlie Carrington acknowledged that you all know each other which triggered a giant red flag.

The messages all have a similar theme and that is the killings are being done as acts of revenge. The actual messages were these," as Jake held up a large piece of construction paper with the four messages.

THE KILLING HAS BEGUN
REVENGE IS MINE
TURN THE OTHER CHEEK? KATAKIUCHI
AN EYE FOR AN EYE

Blake and Kendra Kingston walked into the room at that point and Mrs. Kingston, seeing the message: *"An eye for an eye"* immediately broke down. Reed went over to greet them, gently put his arm around the distraught woman, and whispered softly to her. A moment later she had composed herself and she and her husband sat down. Another brief round of instructions took place and then Reed continued.

"Naturally, since the notes all have a similar message, and since we are now informed that the four fathers know one another, we felt it was crucial to get you all here and to find out who else might be in jeopardy."

"Why do you feel anyone else is in jeopardy?" asked Charlie Carrington. "Or perhaps, I should say, what's to keep this sick bastard from killing forever until he's caught?"

"The clues in the messages point to a specific number, a number we believe to be seven," responded Reed, "and we need to save those three lives."

"What does Katakiuchi mean?" asked Wayne Porter.

"Wiz," why don't you handle this one," said Reed

Wiz again went through the Samurai explanation to the quiet room and when he was through Reed asked, "Gentlemen, in order to help catch the man who killed your children, and hopefully save other parents from going through your pain, we need some answers. I'll begin with: When did you meet?"

The men all looked at each other as if to determine who would be the spokesperson and after an awkward pause Blake Kingston spoke up. "We met our freshman year at Bowdoin - 1983 I believe."

"Yea, that's right," confirmed Charlie Carrington. "We were all in the same freshman dorm - Hastings Hall - and before long we just started hanging out together. We had similar interests, you know, girls, the Red Sox ..."

"Were you roommates?" asked Jake.

"Blake and I were," answered Carrington. "Wayne and Morty had other roommates that year."

"It's my understanding," asked Reed, walking slowly around the room, "that it was only that one year that all four of you were at Bowdoin. Is that right?"

"That's right," began Carrington before Reed cut him off.

"If it's alright, Mr. Carrington, I'd like to hear it from each individual."

"Fine, I graduated from Bowdoin in 1987," he replied without a hint of embarrassment from being cut off.

"I dropped out of school after my freshman year - to find myself," said Ben Mortensen. "I worked odd jobs for the year and then enrolled nights at Framingham State. I graduated in 1989."

"Mr. Porter?" asked Reed

"I just felt it was too difficult," said Wayne Porter. "I wasn't very mature and didn't feel like putting in all that time studying so I transferred after my freshman year to USM and wound up graduating in 1988"

It was Blake Kingston's turn. "I also left after my freshman year. It was just too expensive for my parents so I went home to Vermont and attended Lyndon State – graduated in '87."

"So, only Mr. Carrington graduated from Bowdoin?" asked Walt Wizkowski. You said 1987, I believe, yet your daughter's 23rd birthday was the day that she was killed if I remember correctly."

"Yes," Carrington replied, while his wife put her head down. Lisa got pregnant and we had Angela my sophomore year. Her parents let us move into a small apartment they owned in Topsham although she stayed with them most of the time, both while she was pregnant and during the baby's first year, so I could study."

The next few minutes were spent discussing relationships, children, their parents, and their employment history. Since the other three wives met their future husbands after they left Bowdoin the direction of the conversation seemed to stray.

Each of the detectives had a chance to ask several questions and finally Reed took control once again by raising his voice slightly. "The last couple of questions I need to ask again and I'd like you to think carefully before answering. Is there any reason why you four have been singled out? Did you piss off some class mate, get in a fight in a bar or steal some guys term paper? Can you think of anything that might make someone want to seek revenge?"

Charlie Carrington responded quickly with a firm, "NO. Nothing like that happened." Jake watched as the others nodded slowly in agreement and then asked, "Is there anyone else who hung around with you four - any roommate or friend - someone whose child might be in grave danger?"

Again Carrington responded in the negative.

Reed, frustrated that seemingly there was no breakthrough in missing information, checked to make sure that each of the parents still had the business card with his office and cell numbers that he had handed out when meeting with them earlier. He then asked each of them to complete a questionnaire supplying pertinent contact numbers.

"I'd like to thank you for taking the time to meet with us tonight and please, if anything develops or you remember anything that is pertinent to the case, please call me. Anytime, day or night."

The parents and other detectives had all gone while Jake and Reed stayed behind to pick up the room, gather the information sheets and check at the desk to see if there were any charges. The girl at the desk assured Reed that there was no cost - they were glad to help the State

Police, and the two walked out into the blue-black winter night. When they reached their vehicles in the parking lot Reed hit the remote car door opener and stopped to say what was on his mind. "I'll tell you what, Jake, old buddy. I believe that there is something rotten in Denmark - and I don't mean Denmark, Maine. I can't put my finger on it but after listening to them this evening, I don't believe they're telling the truth."

~ 50 ~

Jake put his foot up on the rear bumper of his car and wrung his hands together as if he was molding pottery. His face, too, showed anxiety, his considerable brows furled. "I understand exactly what you're saying. You're telling me that all four students who have been killed are children of friends of one another and yet they think it's coincidental. *I don't think so,* he said, letting his sarcasm accent the last word as if it had multiple "o's." How in the world did we not see the correlation between these four?"

"Actually, it's really kind of simple," Reed responded, "although all four attended the same college, only one of them graduated from there and three of the four moved out of state. Only Wayne Porter remained in Maine."

"The question I have is why, after one or two of their children were killed, did *they* not see some kind of pattern?"

"Jake, what pattern? The year they attended Bowdoin College together, 1983, there were over 500 other freshmen in that class. Obviously there are lots of children around who had parents attending Bowdoin in 1983."

"But," Jake re-affirmed, "only seven who pissed off our boy to the point where he'd want to kill *their* children."

"Whatta ya think Jake, ... stop at Jimmy D's for a beer? ... it'll give us a chance to talk."

"We could talk in the car or in a library, but if you insist. The food is excellent there I'm told."

"Of course it is. Finest cheeseburgers this side of Harmon's. Do you suppose John Belushi works out back at Jimmy's... cheeseburger...cheeseburger...cheeseburger..."

~ 51 ~

The Painter drove the white van slowly through the streets of Lewiston and Auburn. Known as the twin-cities, albeit miniature versions of Minneapolis-St.Paul, these two mill towns had gone through a major reclamation over the past decade and offered local citizens a variety of quaint restaurants, dance clubs and sports bars at which to congregate.

He was not looking for any of the above but rather was on yet another scouting mission. He had followed his prey from Mac's Steak House to Gipper's, a sports bar with its requisite fifty nine beers on tap and three dozen big screen televisions. *Is it essential,* he thought to himself, *for anyone to follow the fortunes of all those sports teams?*

The victim-to-be was sitting at the bar sipping his second Long Island iced tea - 'hold the Tequila' - while speaking with both the bartender and a female of approximately the same age - barely legal.

Andrew LaFleur was his name, which meant "the flower" in French and he truly was that in the eyes of The Painter. Several other young people of both genders came and went speaking briefly to Andy, paying homage as it were to one of the better known and better liked individuals in the twin cities.

There are those in any community who take umbrage with young people from families of wealth and status who are raised with silver spoons and then handed sinecures above those who broke in on the ground floor. Although Andy, his appellation of choice, was the son of Wallace LaFleur, President of Androscoggin Manufacturing, and grandson of Henri LaFleur, creator of same, he had the good sense to not flaunt his position and a good nature that made those around him comfortable.

Unfortunately for him, The Painter was neither attracted to his good looks or lineage. He was only attracted to studying his habits and habitat. As always, he would analyze where, what, and when Andy went about his business of pleasure so there would be no glitches in the plan.

'The Voice' would be proud. *Yet again!*

~ 52 ~

Reed and Jake walked into Jimmy D's, the ambience of familiarity washing over them. They waved to patrons they recognized from a distance, spoke to those on the bar stools nearby, and on their way to their favorite booth down back their eyes met those of the owner. "Evening Jim," said Reed.

"Say, hey, Jimmy boy," offered Jake with a faux salute ... "what's new?"

"Hey Reed, ... Jake the Snake... New York, New Delhi, and knew your mother intimately... what'll it be fellas?"

"Two black and tans, Jim. What's good on the menu tonight?"

"Cheeseburgers are especially good I'm told."

"We'll take four of your finest Jim, - ketchup and onions."

"Good choice, fellas. I'll be right down."

The men removed their coats, shook a light snow covering from their raiments, and settled into a booth. They had barely been seated when Jimmy placed two black and tans in front of them.

Jimmy, acknowledging the serious look on their faces, said, "No luck yet guys – catching The Painter?"

Reed took a deep gulp of the dark liquid and replied, "No, Jim. It's very frustrating ... and tiring."

"That, my friend," Jimmy countered, "Is why God invented alcohol."

As Jimmy walked away Jake shook his head slowly and said to Reed, "Did you ever wonder if we've got it backwards? We work day and night surrounded by death, destruction and despair trying to make a difference in society and we're criticized, ostracized and shot at. I'm convinced Jimmy has more fun, more friends, and probably puts more smiles on people's faces in a day than we can in a week."

"I'm sure it's the cheeseburgers," Jake. "Now, let's get to the talkin' part."

"Okay, you said when we were leaving the meeting that you didn't believe the men were telling the truth. What makes you say that?"

"Just my gut instincts. Some things just don't make sense to me."

"Like what?"

"Well, the fact that four men, who went one year of college together and then transferred, have remained close all these years. Hell, I went through all four years of college with bunches of guys who I studied with, drank with, and played sports with, and I have no idea where they are today. There must have been something that forced that group to bond."

"Something?"

"Something significant. In order for someone to kill their children - and then leave messages telling us that it's revenge driven, tells us that something pretty serious happened to someone. Also, don't you find it odd that three of the four guys transferred out of Bowdoin - to go to schools - Lyndon State, Framingham, USM, that are clearly not as good academically as Bowdoin – and all after just one year. It seems to me that it's just too much of a coincidence. Lastly, there's something about Charlie Carrington that just doesn't sit well with me. He wanted to answer all of the questions for everybody."

"You don't think that it's just his pushy personality?"

"He's certainly pushy alright, but I felt it was more than that. Almost like he wanted to answer before anyone else got a chance to respond."

"You think we should talk with the others individually?" asked Jake.

"I've thought about that," admitted Reed. Why don't you, Wiz and I each take one of the others to call tomorrow evening after work."

"That's fine, Reed, but wouldn't it be better to speak with them when the wives aren't around? The women clearly aren't involved and we might learn more."

"Good point, Jake. That makes a lot of sense. We'll call them at work tomorrow. We have their numbers on the information cards they filled out."

At that point Jimmy appeared with the cheeseburgers and laid them before the men like the wise men bestowing myrrh upon baby Jesus.

"Eat hardy lads, 'tis food of the Gods."

"Well in that case Jimmy we better have two more drinks - we can't let these brave offerings dine alone," said Jake, "it would be sacrilegious."

~ 53 ~

At the sound of footsteps The Painter sat up, his every nerve ending registering a call to order. He was at the beck and call of 'The Voice' and when he heard the lock on his door open he stood as he had been taught long ago.

"Shower time," the voice announced.

He slid his underwear off his hips and down over his legs leaving him naked in the basement room. Although he knew what was coming he refused to flinch. A cold hand wrapped around his penis and he felt himself being led out of the musty chamber. His hood remained fastened around his neck and even though he couldn't see he knew that they would turn left out of his area and advance through the subterranean chamber for several seconds. He hastened to keep up as the pressure on his penis intensified if he lagged behind.

After reaching their destination he held his hands in front of him as handcuffs were applied to his wrists. His arms were then extended upward where the cuffs were fastened to something above his head. Next, he felt smooth leather straps wrapped around his ankles which served to spread his legs. He was now at the complete mercy of 'The Voice.'

Engulfed in total darkness, his senses wired by the memory of past experiences, The Painter first heard, then felt, the sting of water being applied to his body from a hose. Beginning with a powerful stream directed at the back of his head and back he was soon unhooked from above and told to bend over. After a lengthy assault on his buttocks and legs he was re-fastened and subjected to streams under his arms and then onto his face and below until the jet was aimed at his genitals. The pain was intense as the pressure pounded against his scrotum, his testicles climbing inside his abdomen to escape the onslaught.

At last it was over and a deep breath escaped his lungs. Cold, wet hands began their ministrations on his genitals and soon his testicles dropped from their hiding place. The manual attention continued and he felt himself growing desirous of release. A hand traced his scrotum and along his prostrate until it formed an O and squeezed his shaft.

The Painter leaned his head back anticipating the climax that he felt bubbling within but then a tight rubber elastic was placed over the scrotal sac causing him to gasp.

"Poor baby. Momma didn't let you have any satisfaction," 'The Voice' said as the pain of the aborted release began to throb.

He didn't reply but merely nodded.

"Typical male, thinking with your dick," he heard 'The Voice' snarl as she used the back of her hand to slap his penis with all her might. The pain was considerable but nothing like the time she immersed it in a sleeve of ice and left him hanging.

Again she began to gently rub him bringing pleasure once more.

"Does baby like this?" she asked. "Does baby like being played with?"

Before he could respond she grasped his penis with her fingertips sinking her nails into the soft flesh and causing drops of blood to form where she had squeezed. He let out a muffled groan as he fought to maintain his composure.

"Serves you right, you stupid bastard. So proud of what's hanging between your legs as if it's a divine key to the kingdom - a magical tool designed to provide infinite pleasure to the fair maidens of the land. BULLSHIT! ...You'll use that thing to piss with and only to piss with. If I so much as think you're putting that inside someone while you're out doing my work I'll cut it off. Do you understand?"

The Painter, who had been released from his bondage, knew better than to speak, but nodded feverishly.

~ 54 ~

After being led back into his compound The Painter kneeled down and awaited his directions. It was not long in coming but the tone was remarkably different. A soft, comforting sound resonated throughout the basement. "You have done a wonderful job thus far and our work is almost done. I know you have been following our next target and it is my expectation that you are properly prepared to carry out the next step in our plan. Is that correct?"

The Painter nodded affirmation but that wasn't enough for 'The Voice.' "I can't hear you," came the demand.

"Yes"

"Am I to assume that you have all the necessary items to carry out the task and have taken all of the necessary precautions?"

"Yes"

"Good, and have you decided upon an appropriate time and killing field?"

"Yes"

"What is your plan?"

"On Friday nights he always goes to Gipper's Sports Bar and is the last to leave. He arrives home around 1:15 and this is ideal because where he lives is well shielded and secluded. He has no family and no roommates so unless he brings a girl home with him he will be alone. He will have been drinking and will be unsuspecting. I will park down the road from his house and wait in the hedge that runs beside his driveway. Rather than try to get inside his home, I will take him in the driveway when he steps out of his car. I have already written the note with the message that you gave me and I will kill him per your instructions."

"Wonderful. Since this is Thursday I will speak with you tomorrow to give you the final information. Everything has come together beautifully. It has been just as I hoped and I have planned something special for our next target. Our next victim, the next piece of the puzzle - Andrew LaFleur."

~ 55 ~

Sandy flitted about the kitchen like a worker bee in a hive. He had been up for several hours and prepared the fixings for omelet's, made coffee, and taken Barney for a walk. He had wakened Scott and was reading the morning newspaper when Reed walked into the kitchen, his arms extended over his head, stretching.

"Morning, Sandy," said Reed. "What's new in the Portland Press? Anything I should be aware of?"

"I only read the sports pages - you know, man's accomplishments and, oh yes, my horoscope. It's a five star day for me. I'm to 'rethink a long-term decision,' 'pull away from negativity,' 'curb spending,' and tonight, 'zero in on what I want.'"

"Sounds confusing."

"Not really. I figure if I go easy in the morning, relax after lunch, take a nap in the afternoon, and go to bed early I will have accomplished my goals."

"And how, I ask, is that different than any other of your so-called 'dynamic' days'?" asked Reed.

"The difference, my good man, is that I am being directed, given permission if you will," replied Sandy. "The Gods, recognizing my laborious efforts, are granting me a respite. Who am I to question such cosmic sagacity?"

Reed attempted to keep a straight face but after looking at Sandy he broke into a huge grin and shook his head. "You are something else."

"Speaking of something else, would you like a cup of jamoke, Reed, and how about an omelet? I've got all the fixins' ready for a 'Sandy Special.'"

"No thanks to the omelet Sandy, but I will take the coffee. That is if it doesn't interfere with your divine destiny of inactivity."

Scott walked in, his hair askew, wearing jeans with holes in both knees and a gray athletic t-shirt frayed at the neck. "Good morning Dad, Sandy."

"Good morning, my son," said Reed. "Whatever happened to the age old concept of 'dress for success?'"

"Everybody wears this stuff, Dad. I'm just being fashionable."

"In that case, the homeless people living under a bridge are down right resplendent, I guess."

Sandy interjected saying, "Leave him be, Reed. Times have changed. The Little Lord Faunterloy look is out - although you did look spiffy in your Buster Browns as I remember."

"What are Buster Browns, asked Scott?"

"Shoes, Scotty. Cadillacs for the feet," replied Reed."

Sandy stood and sprayed Pam into a frying pan asking Scott, "What would you like in your omelet?"

"The usual I guess. Ham, mushrooms, onions and of course, cheese."

Sandy put on his apron that read 'World's Best Grandpa' that the boys had given him two birthdays ago and said, "Of course. Put melted cheese on anything and it's delicious. I once had a college friend who said melted cheese on door knobs would be worth eating."

"I wish I could stay and chat," said Reed as he downed the last sip of coffee, "but I've got to get ready and go to the barracks."

"It's been real and it's been fun but I'm not sure it's been real fun," said Sandy from the stove, harkening back to sophomoric humor of the past.

Reed just shook his head and walked into the bathroom. He had just completed covering his face with shaving cream when his cell phone rang. Putting it next to his ear he heard a male voice that he had heard before but failed to recognize.

"Sergeant Sanderson?"

"Yes, Who is this?"

"Wayne Porter, Sergeant. I'm sorry to call you so early but I need to speak with you."

"That's okay, Wayne, what is it?"

"When we spoke to you recently …we…we…didn't …we didn't tell the truth."

~ 56 ~

"I'm sorry, I'm not sure that I heard you," replied Reed, wiping shaving cream from his phone.

"I said, this is Wayne Porter and when we met with you recently we did not tell you the truth, or at least all of the truth. More importantly, as you suggested, there is someone else who was friendly with us who should be warned."

"Wayne, where are you now?"

"I'm home in Windham."

"Listen, it will take 10-15 minutes for me to get there. Don't leave, I'm out the door."

Buttoning his shirt while he walked through the kitchen, Reed leaned in to kiss Scott on the top of his head saying, "Have a great day. I've got to run to meet with a key witness but hopefully I'll be home for supper. Bending over he patted Barney as well.

"Good luck, Dad."

"Sandy, I'll call you. I'd run my hand through your hair but I'd probably just mess up your Brylcream."

"What's Brylcream, Sandy?" asked Scott as Reed headed out the door.

Reed was unable to reach Jake but left a message and did get in touch with Walt Wizkowsi and Tom Lombardo who agreed to join him. Each of the detectives headed directly for the Porter home. Because he was convinced that the life of one or more students may be in jeopardy Reed turned on his siren and flashing wig-wags coming down Route 302 into Windham and it saved him several minutes. He felt his heart beating rapidly in his chest as he drove into the desired driveway where the other two men were waiting for Reed outside.

They found Wayne Porter nervously pacing the floor when they walked in and it was reflected in the telling of his admission, "I, …we, …didn't tell the truth the other night when we got together," he began, and then paused. He rubbed both hands through his hair and then began again. "In fact, … we do have an idea of what is going on … but we, … I, … never thought this would happen. …Oh my poor Dee Dee," he sobbed, tears running down his face, voice cracking. … "I should have known."

"Known what, Wayne?" asked Reed gently yet with a hint of exasperation.

"It all happened so long ago - when we were young and full of piss and vinegar," he began, as if the story to come was going to be both long and convoluted.

Reed, sensing that, interrupted. "Wayne, excuse me for interrupting - and we do need to hear the whole story - but on the phone you said there was someone else who you were involved with and who should be warned - who is that? Let us alert him and provide coverage so that no one else gets killed."

"Oh, oh, yes, certainly," stuttered Porter. "Contact Wallace LaFleur in Lewiston. He was one of us and he has a son."

"Do you have a phone number for Wallace LaFleur?" asked Wizkowski.

"No, but he can be reached at Androscoggin Manufacturing. He's the President."

Reed spoke to the pair of detectives in the living room. "Wiz, you get ahold of Wallace LaFleur and tell him the circumstances. Tom, you get the name, number and location of his son and put a tail on him. Also get in touch with the Chief of Police in Lewiston, Frank Fennessey, and let him in on our situation – and gentlemen, do not breathe a word of this to anyone in the media. I will stay with Wayne and hopefully get some more information that might be useful."

There was an instant surge in activity as both men headed for their respective cars and phones.

"Now, Wayne," continued Reed. "What did you mean by the comment, 'he was one of us?'"

~ 57 ~

"It goes back to our freshman year at Bowdoin, Sergeant Sanderson - back to 1983. There were five of us who arrived on campus, all from different locations and backgrounds, who were put in the same wing of Hastings Hall."

"Before long we were hanging out together, studying together, going places together. The five of us were virtually inseparable and that's when we got the idea of giving ourselves a name ... a kind of nickname for our little group. We called ourselves D2MAD and even had tee-shirts made up with that slogan on it."

"People would ask what it stood for, what it meant, but we swore not to reveal it... unless a girl agreed to sleep with all five of us. Then, not only would we tell her what the message stood for, but we also agreed that we would give the girl one of our tee-shirts."

"It only happened on two occasions. The first shirt went to Becky Davis, a cheerleader who was gorgeous and had an insatiable sexual appetite. We didn't care. We were just your typical horny freshmen who would show up at some frat house or dorm on weekends and try to talk a co-ed into coming back to our dorm room with us. I guess the phrase today is "hooking up" ... that's what Dee Dee told me," ...and here he stopped to regain his composure.

"I'm sorry, Wayne but we ..."

"No one uses 'co-ed' anymore either but the fact is that Charlie Carrington finally got Becky over Winter Carnival weekend and she became the first to get a shirt. She was embarrassed at first when we told her what the criteria was to have received it, but before long we saw her wearing it around campus like it was special. It was kind of big on her, we only ordered X-L's, but we hoped that she would explain to other girls on campus how she had 'earned' it and there would be a competitive clamoring. Guess we were pretty naïve, huh?" he said with a wry smile.

"I don't mean to intercede in your trip down nostalgia lane," said Reed, "but so far I don't see any connection to the murders."

"Well," answered Wayne, "that's where the only other recipient of our tee-shirt comes into play - she earned it all in one night."

~ 58 ~

"She what?" asked Reed.

She earned her tee-shirt in one night," responded Wayne. "One night in the spring we all went over to the apartment in Topsham where Charlie was living. His girlfriend, now wife, must have been at her parents home because we were sitting around watching a ballgame, having a few beers. We were kinda bored when Wally, who had more money than the rest of us combined, suggested that we hire a dancer to come over and provide a little entertainment."

"By Wally, you mean Wallace LaFleur?" asked Reed.

"Yes."

"So what happened?"

"Wally offered to pay for the girl coming over to dance and looked up the number of an escort place in the phone book."

"Do you remember the name of the place?"

"It was 'something Pleasures,' I think, but we didn't care and never had enough money to use them anyway …just Wally, and I heard some of the fraternities would hire a girl occasionally."

"Go on."

"So, about an hour later this pretty dark-haired babe with great tits showed up at the apartment."

"Do you remember her name?"

"She called herself Vicki but I have no idea what her real name was."

"Okay, what's next?"

"Well, by now we were pretty well loaded so when this babe starts to take off her clothes it didn't take us long to get fired up - and, boys being boys, - one thing led to another. Before we knew it we were hot to trot."

"The girl, who said she was working her way through college, didn't intend to do anything but dance but when Wally offered her fifty dollars extra to take her top off - she went along with it. She had a couple of beers with us and danced topless for awhile."

"I'm guessing it didn't end there," said Reed.

"No, but we sure wish it had. Wally offered her a hundred dollars to take her bottoms off and she made us promise that that was all… but you know how these things go. By now we were shit-faced and we all wanted to screw her. Wally offered her $200 but she refused saying that she was a dancer, not a whore. At that point we didn't see the difference and Wally wasn't going to take 'no' for an answer. So he slid his pants down and told us to hold her down on the floor."

"He climbed on top of her and the rest of us were feeling her up and holding her down. She started screaming so Charlie slapped her across the face and told her to 'shut her fucking mouth'. He held up a bottle opener and said 'you scream once more and that pretty face of yours won't be so pretty.'"

"After Wally got done with her Charlie climbed on and he had his way with her as well. The rest of us were still holding her down. We poured a couple more beers down her throat and she finally stopped putting up a fight. After Charlie got done he suggested that this would be a great opportunity for another woman to earn a D2MAD tee-shirt so the other three of us screwed her as well."

"It was after we were all done and she was lying there whimpering that Wally decided he was going to do her with a beer bottle. He was still pissed off that she wouldn't do it with him when he offered her money – he was used to getting what he wants, you know, even then."

"No, I do not know. I am not familiar with him at all," Reed responded to the rhetorical question.

"Well, he did - and does, I'm told."

"Get back to your story."

"Well, when the babe heard Wally talking about using a beer bottle she went ballistic and started throwing things. Wally, who was pretty messed-up by then, threw a punch at the girl, split her lip, and momentarily dazed her. He ordered us to once again hold her down so we each grabbed a leg or arm and he rammed the beer bottle up inside of her. She was spitting blood, swearing at us and thrashing around fit to be tied. Hell, if we'd had a rope, we would have used it I'm sure."

"Wally kept jamming that bottle inside her saying, 'the little bitch loves it. She can't get enough of it.' When he got done with her there was blood everywhere and she had passed out. We weren't sure if it was from the beers or the pain but we knew we had to get out of there. By now Charlie had come to his senses and kept saying, 'We can't let Lisa find out - Lisa will kill me.'"

Reed, who had listened attentively to Wayne's story and taken copious notes, felt revulsion at what he'd just heard and anger that he was just now hearing it. He realized just how damning this story was to those involved but also knew there must be more to the story than that which he had just heard. "So what happened to the girl?" he asked.

"We wrapped her up in a blanket with her clothes and carried her out to her car. We threw a D2MAD t-shirt in the back seat and then went back inside to clean up the mess. When we were all done the car was gone. We never heard from her again."

Reed was now standing making notes in the pad resting on his bent knee. "I am sure there is a great deal more to hear," he said to Wayne Porter. "By the way, what does 'D2MAD' stand for?"

Wayne's face held an embarrassed grin as the words were released from his lips - 'Determined to Make a Difference,' he said.

"That's just beautiful," Reed said sarcastically as he shook his head. "You certainly did."

~ 59 ~

The sun was just peeking over the horizon as an assemblage of state troopers ascended on the three-story clapboard building. Reed and Jake were in the lead patrol car followed by several others arriving both behind them and coming in from the opposite direction.

They quietly exited the Crown Vics and Impalas and Reed silently pointed to several of the officers, instructing them to proceed stealthily around the perimeter of the building covering all of the potential exit points. Reed, Jake and four others would enter the front door and proceed to the second floor apartment.

Following the visualization of the license plate on the black Escalade earlier at Jake's condo Reed had run a registration inquiry and had found a match with a Joseph Mercier who was listed as residing in Apartment 2 at 410 Lisbon Street in Lewiston. They had decided to make an early-morning visit in hopes of returning the favor afforded Jake.

Reed stopped to take a good look at the building that they were about to enter. The run down structure had paint peeling off, a gutter hanging loosely down on one side and a metal fire escape that had steps missing. Several of the windows were cracked and those which apparently were to the basement, were missing altogether. On one side of the building a dirt driveway served as parking for the residents. There were several tired, old and rusty vehicles cluttering up the side yard but there was no sign of a black Cadillac Escalade.

Despite the earliness of the hour Reed headed into the building with a fervor that only adrenalin can provide. The building had only one internal stairway and the officers climbed slowly trying not to alert the inhabitants by stepping heavily on the squeaky floor boards and steps.

When they reached the second floor the six fanned out with three on each side of the door marked #2 and waited for the command from Reed. He placed his ear to the wall outside the door but heard no signs of movement inside. After pausing for several seconds he beckoned to the troopers holding the "enforcer," a door-opening battering ram, and then dropped his hand. Because they had received a "no-knock warrant" from a District Court Judge they did not need to verbally announce their presence and the troopers charged the obstacle. The flimsy door splintered under the assault and the supporting officers rushed in, weapons drawn.

It took only a matter of seconds to check each of the five rooms and ascertain they were vacant. A collection of empty pizza boxes lay scattered around the bedrooms. When Reed kicked one aside a cock roach the size of a half-dollar scurried toward the safety of a closet. Beer cans and pornographic magazines were the only other vestiges of former occupation in the bedrooms and the entire furnishings consisted of two cots, a ratty sofa with a hole in one side and a small black and white television with rabbit ears resting on an orange crate.

Reed just shook his head as he looked around the squalid surroundings. If Mercier or anyone else had lived here recently, he thought, it sure didn't take long for them to pack and "tidy up."

Jake was updating the troopers outside while Reed and a couple of others went through the apartment looking for anything that might be useful. It had only been a couple of minutes when Reed sounded out. Holding a piece of yellow-lined paper that he had found in one of the kitchen cabinets he read the message, written in pencil, to his partner. It made the hairs on the back of his neck stand up.

"Nice try Jake – see you soon."

~ 60 ~

Reed sent most of the troopers back while he, Jake, and several other of the detectives went door to door interviewing the tenants of the Lewiston apartment house.

They learned that two brothers had lived in Apartment #2 but they had not been seen in several days. Most informative was the conversation with Will Archambeault, a mechanic who lived across the hall from the brothers in Apartment #1.

A tall, skinny man with hollow cheeks and vacant eyes, he was roused by the early morning episode and answered the detectives questions reluctantly. "I ain't got no idea where they went. I last seen them about 4-5 days ago and they ain't been back since.

Jake continued the questioning, "Do you know what their names are?" he asked.

"No idea, but I heard the smaller one call the bigger one 'Snake.'"

"What did they look like?"

"Snake is a big bastard. Must go six foot three, two eighty. Bald as a bat with two gold earrings. The other one was muscular but shorter. He had a handle bar moustache and generally wore a black leather jacket. Snake usually had a jean jacket on. I didn't want to mess with either one of 'em. Say, what have they done, anyway?"

"How long have they lived here?" Reed continued, ignoring the question.

"Couple months."

"What do they drive," asked Jake.

"Nice wheels," replied Archambeault, "black Caddy SUV."

Reed looked at Jake without saying anything. "Did they have jobs?"

"No idea, but I doubt it. They just kinda came and went at all hours. They weren't much for talking. The only conversation we had was when they first moved in. They asked me if I wanted to buy some weed. I told 'em I didn't use that shit and that was that. That's probably how they make their money."

"Did you see them have any company?"

"Just once. A whole buncha guys came in a few days ago. Several were on motorcycles which is how I knew. I was trying to sleep when I heard their bikes and then they came clumping up the stairs. I didn't open my door but I could sure as shit hear them in there – drinkin', hooting', hollerin'. I was pissed but I didn't want no trouble so I didn't fuck with 'em."

"So you didn't see what any of these others looked like, you know, young, old, men, women?"

"Like I told ya' I didn't open the door. I never heard any women's voices though. Oh, one other thing. As they were leaving – it was 3:15 a.m. and I was still awake - I heard one of 'em holler, 'We'll see you boys Saturday at the pit'. Is that of any help?"

"It may be Mr. Archambeault," answered Reed taking a card out of his wallet. "It just may be. Say, if those boys should return to their apartment would you mind giving me a call?"

After comparing notes with the other detectives and gathering all of the information Reed and Jake got back into their car and headed back to Gray.

"What do you make of all this, Reed?"

"Well, it sure seems personal with that note addressed to you. They obviously have done their homework and as I said to you before, you had best be careful. These boys have proven that they don't fool around. I got the name of the apartment owner but I'm sure we won't learn a great deal from him. They probably used an alias to rent and I doubt they'll come back to this apartment. I'm amazed they used their real name and address when registering their vehicle."

"Don't worry about me. Do you think Archambeault was on the up and up?"

"He seemed to be. I've got an idea he's had run-ins with the law before. We'll run a check on him. More importantly, what he overheard may be of value. I've got an idea that 'The Pit' is the old Morgan gravel pit in Greene. You know, where we've been called in because there's been kids drinking up there. I suggest that we investigate a bit more and then pay them a visit. Since tomorrow is Saturday we need to act quickly. If there turns out to be a skinhead convention then this exercise may not prove to have been a waste of time after all."

~ 61 ~

Reed received the phone call just before dusk from a trooper who had been dropped off above Morgan's gravel pit several hours earlier with instructions to serve as a sentry and notify him at the first indication of activity.

For this operation Reed had commandeered all 23 members of the State's Tactical Team including two k-9's and two medics. Specially trained, the Tactical Unit worked in conjunction with the State Police's Crisis Negotiation Team and generally responded to over four dozen incidents per year since it had been formed in 1982.

The troopers, who came from all over the State, were meeting at the barracks in Gray, several minutes from the gravel pit, where they were being briefed on their assignments and potential problems. Jake, who had researched the white supremacist movement in Maine, provided an overview: "Most of these hate groups are regional in nature and we believe the group that we are monitoring is a splinter organization that call themselves East Coast White Unity. The ECWU broke away from the North East White Pride and, while they are predominantly based outside of Boston, there is an ever-growing gang here in Maine that was founded a couple of years ago by a man named Joseph Mercier. His father died from a heart attack while attending a KKK rally and he is thought to be the one who killed Reed's son, Tommy, thinking it was me. I threw the old man up against a car when things got chaotic in that Lewiston rally and Joseph, who goes by the nickname, 'Snake,' must want retribution. These groups hold monthly meetings and are constantly trying to recruit new 'losers' to their hate organizations. Make no mistake. Although they are not breaking any law by meeting, this is a dangerous group. We must take every precaution."

"Thanks Jake", Reed continued. "Earlier Jake and I visited the location to get a 'lay of the land.' Comprising almost 20 acres, the pit has one major entrance large enough for the trucks that carried thousands of loads out of the site when it was active, and a smaller secondary road opposite. There is a drop in elevation of seventy feet from the entrance to the bottom of the pit and the gouge is divided by a wall of ledge that offers refuge for those who want to have target practice, under age parties, or gatherings. We have information that leads us to believe that the ECWU is meeting today at this pit."

The trooper on guard duty called back to report that the gathering now numbered several dozen and in addition to a large bon fire there were different individuals taking turns addressing the group. From his vantage point above he could see there was a lot of drinking and the smell of marijuana hung heavily in the air.

Reed did not want to arrive too soon feeling that there would be safety, both in the fall of darkness as well as what he hoped, would be some degree of impairment, following the use of drugs and alcohol.

Finally, just before ten o' clock, Reed and the rest of the Tactical Unit arrived at the pit and as previously discussed divided their number between the two access roads. Like well-dressed ninjas they sported camouflage clothing, advanced combat helmets with riot face shields and Level II Kevlar body vests. Each trooper was carrying a Heckler&Koch MP5, a sub-machine gun popular for its size and light weight and used by law enforcement agencies in over forty countries.

While it may have seemed to some that they were being overly cautious in regard to their choice of clothing and weapons, Reed knew how very dangerous this group could be and hoped that this show of force would serve as a deterrent. If it did not, then they were prepared for whatever ensured. After all, not only had one of them killed his son, but they had also engineered a night-time raid on Jake's condo.

Reed focused his binoculars on the group below, most of whom were gathered around the large fire. He could see that many were bald and several had placards on which were written various hate messages. Scanning to the opposite side of the cliff, where the skinheads had parked, Reed could see there were dozens of motorcycles, an assortment of varying types of pick-ups and automobiles and one black Cadillac Escalade.

It had been determined that the Tactical Team would descend upon the gathering along with Reed and Jake while other troopers would provide support above. After the advance team had begun the climb down the embankment a flat-bed truck would be placed across each road where it leveled off sealing off potential escape routes.

Reed was in charge of the descent into the side of the pit where the vehicles were parked while Niko Lascinetta, a tactical trooper from Turner, was in charge of the opposite side where the skinheads had congregated. The plan was to surround the gathering without their knowledge and, by demonstrating a significant police presence, hopefully limit the amount of retaliation by the militant group. The assumption was that many, if not all of them, had weapons on or near them and there was an extreme need for caution.

Reed, equipped with a throat mike, whispered to Niko on the other side of the pit, "We're in position and good to go."

Niko responded in like fashion, "We are too. Stay close and proceed slowly."

"When you get to the base of the pit try to spread out if you can. We are going to move in on the vehicles hoping to eliminate any attempts to escape. Remember, we are only after 'Snake" and his brother – and Niko, we want to take them alive so they can be questioned."

"Gotcha, Reed. Let's move."

The clouds covered the moon and the sky looked like molasses as the troopers slowly climbed down the two dirt roads into the pit. When the group on the side of the gathering had reached the bottom and were starting to fan out a shout rang out from one of the skinheads, "LOOK, THERE'S FUCKING COPS BEHIND US!"

All hell broke loose as Niko yelled into a bullhorn, "STOP WHERE YOU ARE. YOU ARE SURROUNDED."

That announcement was met with the sound of gunfire and the skinheads who were not responding with shots, were racing toward their vehicles on the other side of the granite point. Seeing the second wave of troopers in battle gear with weapons drawn caused most of the skinheads to stop and put their hands up in the air. Cries of "Don't Shoot," filled the black night.

Two who did not stop were Snake and his brother. Both sprinted toward their car with the latter firing shots from a pistol while attempting to get into the driver's side of the Escalade. As he swung open the door and placed one foot inside a bullet entered the back of his head sending shards of bone and brain matter into the windshield.

Snake, who saw this as he was entering the passenger side, screamed "NOOO" but did not stop. Instead he ran around the front of the SUV and jumped on one of the off-road motorbikes parked there. He turned the key that had been left in the bike, revved it up, and sped across the pit spewing sand and gravel on those nearest him. A multitude of shots were fired but none made contact with the rider who was now building up considerable speed and heading up the dirt road exit. Two troopers waited, one on each side of the flat bed truck, and Reed watched expecting a terrific crash as the motorcyclist approached the truck.

Instead Reed gazed in amazement as the rider pulled on the front of the bike as he reached the top of the incline and sailed over the flatbed, landing with a thud on the other side. It looked for a moment to the two troopers that he was going to go down but instead he maintained his balance and sped away.

The two troopers assigned to the top jumped into their cruisers and took off after the bike but Reed knew what the outcome of that chase would be. "Can you fucking believe it," he asked to no one in particular.

~ 62 ~

Wallace Charles LaFleur ran Androscoggin Manufacturing like he ran his life. A bull of a man with wide shoulders, wide nostrils and piercing dark green eyes, his voice was more of a stentorian bark than a speech pattern. When he spoke, people listened and most often jumped.

Because he had lost much of his hair at an early age he had made the decision - not to give up on his hair - *Wallace LaFleur did not give up on anything.* Rather, he took control - and shaved his head.

For those old enough to remember Telly Savalas as Kojak the comparison was inevitable, only Telly would smile occasionally and often uttered his catchword phrase, "who loves ya' baby?"

Wallace LaFleur was convinced that smiling was a sign of weakness and, though he had once loved his wife, and worshipped his son Andy, he viewed his employees as chattel and would no more issue a term of endearment than he would hand out a Christmas bonus.

He inherited control of the company from his father, Henri, who was still listed on the books as Chairman Emeritus, when he was twenty-seven and had run the operation with the patience and precision of a drill sergeant.

When Walt Wizkowski walked into LaFleur's office he was taken by the masculine ambience and inordinate sense of organization. It was clear that LaFleur intended there to be no areas of indecision or indecisiveness - no loose ends.

Wizkowski's eyes were immediately drawn to the many photos and plaques lining the walls. It was clearly evident that Wallace LaFleur was a major player in the social, economic and civic scene in the Lewiston-Auburn area.

The man himself rose from behind an expansive mahogany desk replete with family photos and a glass paperweight collection numbering in the dozens.

"Good morning, Detective ... Wizkowski, is it? To what do I owe this honor?" said LaFleur, meaty hand extended.

"Good morning," responded Wizkowski, who had decided not to alarm the man by making a phone call of explanation but, rather, set up a meeting and drove straight there.

"Please be seated, I'm afraid I have some alarming news for you."

"What's that, Officer?"

"Sir, we have every reason to believe that your son's life is in danger and we want to help you, help him."

"What makes you think that his life is in danger, Detective?"

Wizkowski proceeded to recite that which Wayne Porter had told them earlier in the day as LaFleur listened with a modicum of attentiveness. Wizkowski, noticing this, asked the man pointedly, "Mr. LaFleur, you don't seem overly concerned by what I've told you. Is there something I don't know - something you're not telling me?"

"Why no, officer and please don't think for a minute I am not concerned about Andrew. He is the light of my life and, like any parent, I want him to be safe and successful. I appreciate your help, really I do... it's just that I feel that you are being needlessly concerned."

"Let me see if I have this right, Mr. LaFleur. There were five of you at Bowdoin, who all hung out together. The other four have lost a child and yet you think we're being needlessly concerned?" asked Wizkowski incredulously.

"I truly appreciate your coming here today to warn me and I will have a talk with Andrew."

"We have another detective doing that currently, Mr. LaFleur. Tell me, the young lady who you paid to come to the apartment that night - do you remember her name? Did you ever see or speak with her again?"

"No, I don't think so ... why do you ask?"

"It just seems strange," Wizkowski pondered out loud, "that if it happened as Wayne Porter says it happened, there were no further repercussions...no further contact..."

~ 63 ~

Joe Quinn found Andrew LaFleur having breakfast at Sebagle Lake Bagels, a small shop in Gray. It had only taken Quinn two phone calls to find his whereabouts and ten minutes to reach the shop. The petite young lady behind the counter pointed him out to Quinn and he nestled into a booth opposite LaFleur introducing himself in the process.

"Nice to meet you, sir," … stammered LaFleur, not sure of the rank of the trooper in front of him or what to say. "Are you looking for me?"

"Yes, Mr. LaFleur, I am," said Quinn, noticing the striking green eyes, pronounced chin and wavy black hair on the young man.

"Please call me Andy. … What is it you want?… How did you find me?"

"I just want to speak with you for a minute, Andy. I called the factory and a secretary there told me that you might be here."

"I am pretty predictable, I guess," the young man admitted. "They have the best bagels here."

"It's that predictability I want to speak to you about Andy, and the fact that you might be in danger. I'm here to offer some suggestions and some help."

"Danger?" he repeated. "What kind of danger?"

For the second time that day an officer explained to a LaFleur the concerns of the State Police relative to earlier actions and relationships. Quinn felt no need to go into details about the rape as it related to the young man's father but did point out the lack of coincidence in the other four students being murdered. This time the man listened with stark attention and a countenance reflective of the seriousness.

"And you think I might be next," he asked. "I haven't hurt anyone - hell, I don't believe I have any enemies."

Quinn smiled at the young man and was taken by his naivete, "I'm sure you don't, but there seems to be a correlation with the fathers of those young people being killed."

"What do you want from me?" asked Andy, beads of sweat forming on his forehead.

"First of all, I'd like you to become a little less predictable, Andy. We believe the killer stalks his prey and is very well informed - that's why he has been so hard to catch."

"Secondly, I would like you to become very aware of the people around you. Watch to see if someone is watching you or if someone's behavior seems strange to you. Lastly, we intend to put constant surveillance on you until the killer is caught."

"But, I have to go to work."

"By all means," answered Quinn. "I am not saying don't conduct normal activities – just be aware and vary times if possible. We will be around you but will not interfere in your actions. Here is a card with my number on it. Call me at any time if you observe, or even sense, something out of the ordinary."

"Thank you, … and Mr. Quinn, what do I call you?"

"How about early and often, " replied Quinn. "I want to save your life."

~ 64 ~

The Painter grabbed his burlap bag which contained a set of workman overalls, a roll of gray duct tape, a coil of laundry line, several pairs of plastic gloves, the next note to be left at the crime scene and, oh yes, a seven inch knife.

As he perused each of the items inside the bag he couldn't help but compare himself to Santa Claus - making a list and checking it twice. Although he, himself, had never been visited by the fictional character as a youngster, he had read of the customs associated with him. Furthermore, he thought, Andy LaFleur must have been an especially good boy this year since Santa was not only going to visit his house, but Santa had a special treat for Andy this year.

It was Friday and today was the day that he would go hunting. He looked forward to these days, no, he loved these days. It wasn't the actual killing itself, he neither cared nor knew about the targets other than the information gleaned by his surveillance. It was the satisfaction he received from having accomplished his goal that meant the most to him - and the satisfaction from having 'The Voice' praise him for his efforts. Over the years he had come to need this acceptance, this praise.

'The Voice' would provide him the names of the targets and he was allowed to do the rest. He was given the freedom to track the intended victim and learn that person's habits and routines.

From the time years ago when he was taken out on the family farm and taught how to drive the van, he had enjoyed the freedom and excitement of being in his own little world. The fact that his driving ability was home taught, and that he had no license, meant no more to him than being home-schooled all those years. He had been instructed that the world can be a big, dangerous place and he was thankful to 'The Voice' for shielding him from those that would hurt him. She was all that he needed.

He slid the massive wooden door of the barn back on its rusty overhead hinges and climbed into the old white van. As always, it had been scrubbed to an immaculate state and, except for his burlap bag, held nothing. The sun had gone down an hour ago, he noted as he headed down the long dirt driveway into mainstream society. He had been told that they called him The Painter due to the notes he left. He preferred being called "my baby" or "my little man" because of what it meant and from whom it came.

~ 65 ~

The Painter parked his van in the ample parking lot that served Gipper's Sports Bar as well as several other businesses on Route 4 in Auburn. The driving had been uneventful – he knew to 'always go five miles per hour under the speed limit so you won't be stopped.'

He selected a spot a safe distance away from the bar but close enough so he could identify the faces of those inside through the glass. He saw no Mazda RX7 in the parking lot so he knew that Andy LaFleur had not yet arrived, but he was not worried. Death, taxes, and Andy being at Gipper's on Friday nights were as sure as it got.

He would sit quietly and watch the show unfold in the local watering hole; twenty-somethings with nary a thought about the imminence of death. He knew that a cast of characters would come and go and tomorrow, after watching the news or reading the local paper, they would recall in horror, "I was with him just last night," or "I saw him the other night at Gipper's."

He would not do anything near the bar - it was much too risky. No, he would wait until Andy prepared to leave before he would depart and beat him to his house. He would park down the street, secure a safe location in the hedge beside his driveway and surprise the young man as he got out of his car. Neat, clean, precise and predetermined. Just as he liked it.

~ 66 ~

Andy LaFleur left the Prime Time OTB parlor in Lewiston with a smile on his face and an extra sixty bucks in his pocket. He enjoyed frequenting this off-track betting parlor for occasional wagers into harness racing's top tracks; The Meadowlands and Yonkers Raceway.

On this night he had selected an exacta box at Yonkers with one of Maine's finest drivers, Jason Bartlett, getting up for the win. He thought about a sign he had on his desk at work, 'I hope I break even today. I need the money.' That was good for a chuckle but in reality he didn't really *need* the money. He had a great job with a future. After all, he was a LaFleur. It was more of the challenge of picking winners, deciphering the complex numbers on a race program. Winning money was just a vindication, a bonus.

He stopped to imbibe the crisp air. He knew somewhere there was a pair of men following him, watching over him, but he didn't know where and didn't care to look around. He had been concerned when the detective told him that he was in danger but he couldn't comprehend why. He always tried to treat others fairly and with respect. But, Detective Quinn was insistent and he guessed that he felt an added sense of security knowing that he had invisible watchdogs.

Bending to fit his tall frame into the Mazda sports car, he looked in the rearview mirror before pulling out of the parking lot. Shortly thereafter he saw a pair of headlights come on and a dark Chevy Impala pull forward.

It was a short ride to Gipper's Sports Bar and a sense of exhilaration filled him as he walked into the establishment. The smell of popcorn from an old-fashioned cart in the corner filled his nostrils while the sounds of laughter and good cheer reverberated through the large room. He immediately recognized several of the patrons and hands waved for him to join them. He loved frequenting Gippers; it was always full of friendly and familiar faces.

One face that was neither friendly nor familiar leaned forward in his white van. He glanced at the burlap bag in the seat beside him and rubbed his hands together with a sense of anticipation. *It won't be long now.*

~ 67 ~

"Last Call for Alcohol, Andy," a bombshell disguised as a waitress said at about five minutes before one.

"Thanks, Darcy, but I think I've had enough for tonight," answered Andrew LaFleur rubbing his hand through his dark hair. "Let me have my tab please, and Darcy, put the tab of the two girls sitting over there on mine," nodding his head in their direction.

"Sure thing Andy, just give me a minute."

He knew it was late and didn't expect to reap the rewards of his largesse tonight but, he mused, it was seed money.

Darcy returned with his check and walked over to the pair sitting near him; Bates College girls, he guessed. After the waitress spoke briefly to the girls they both waved thanks to him. Normally he would use that as an entrée to an introduction but, instead, he just returned the wave and headed for the door. If they didn't know his name they soon would, either from Darcy or from overhearing the many people who called his name as he departed.

The Painter had not seen any of this as he had left ten minutes earlier. He had already parked his van several hundred yards down the road in a Central Maine Power transformer pull-in. Lined with thin arborvitae bushes they offered some coverage and a passing motorist might incorrectly suspect that a CMP employee was working late. Oh, he was working late, alright, but it wasn't on transformers.

The Painter stepped into the overalls and walked down the dark road, duffel bag in hand. He secured a spot in the hedge of blue spruce trees that touched each other at their bottom third. They had grown to over fifteen feet tall and formed a natural border along the driveway. From his vantage point he estimated that he would be just six to eight feet behind his target after he pulled in and shut off the car, a mere two or three strides.

As LaFleur was getting out of the Mazda he would jump the

unsuspecting young man.

One quick slice across the throat should do the trick and then he would finish his business and be on his way.

~ 68 ~

The Painter tensed as he saw a set of headlights illuminating the distant night. He stepped deeper into the darkness of the tall trees, knife in hand, duffel bag on the ground beside him. As the lights came closer they speared the trees until the car pulled into the driveway sending full rays on the garage ahead, to The Painter's left. He felt prickles of excitement rise on the back of his neck, his palms became sweaty inside the plastic gloves. He crouched, cat-like, waiting for just the right moment to spring.

The Mazda proceeded slowly up the driveway past where he was in hiding and came to a stop even with the back door some ten feet in front of him. The Painter inched closer to the driveway, his muscles taut as he watched the lights go out and heard the metallic click of the driver's door being opened. He bent his knees and advanced in Indian fashion one silent step at a time until he saw the frame of the driver place one foot on the ground and rise from the confines of the bucket seat to a standing position.

The Painter sprang at his target and with his right hand extended lunged toward the back right side of the man. His left arm wrapped around the man's neck as the knife was moved in front of his face with the intent of making a quick cut across the jugular. He did not expect the man to react but he did, dipping his right shoulder throwing both of them into the side of the car. "What the…" was all The Painter could get out as he missed the man's neck but dragged the knife across the man's chest on the right side and through his right bicep. Despite the gaping wound the victim fought to maintain his balance. Unable to use his right side he swung with his left hand, missed, but landed on The Painter pinning him to the ground on his right side and knocking the knife to the ground.

With his right hand being rendered useless The Painter took his left hand and reached up to rake the eye of his combatant. His quick movement caused a dark wig to fall off the man's head and he realized that it was not his intended target, with whom he was grappling, but Reed who was dressed to look like Andy LaFleur.

Another pair of headlights appeared at the end of the driveway as The Painter looked up and saw what he assumed was a police officer jump from the driver's side of an Impala while out from the passenger side stepped Andy LaFleur. Jake Lewis yelled for Andy to "Stay in the car" and hollered at The Painter "Don't Move!"

Undeterred The Painter tightened his headlock grip on Reed taking his breath away. Jake could see that Reed was bleeding profusely and, not knowing the severity of the wounds, needed to act quickly. The Painter edged closer to the knife on the ground keeping Reed's body between him and the detective's gun.

When he was right over the knife he applied more pressure to Reed's neck and slowly dropped to a crouch while pulling Reed backwards. He bent down to pick up the knife but as he did so he momentarily relaxed the grip on Reed's neck. Reed sensed this and threw his elbow into The Painter's stomach. The Painter released his hold on Reed, grabbed for the knife and began to lunge at Reed when a 45 caliber shell entered his neck knocking him backward into the Mazda.

Jake watched The Painter gather himself, the knife now resting in his right hand and stepped toward Reed who was lying on the driveway one stride away from the killer. Jake didn't hesitate. He had no time to threaten the assailant or warn his partner. When he saw The Painter step toward Reed, eyes glazed, blood spurting from the side of his neck, he fired one more round into the chest of the assailant. The knife flew backward as did the man holding it. He slid down the car into a sitting position, legs spread, head cocked to one side. Blood pooled on the driveway from the two mortal wounds. His eyes remained open, dark and vacant.

Jake put down his gun and bent down to administer to his fallen friend. "Reed, hang in there ole buddy," he implored. "We're going to get you some help." His call to dispatch rang through.

"WE HAVE A 1074 ... SEND AN AMBULANCE TO ..."

~ 69 ~

The Lewiston Sun, like all of the daily newspapers, screamed their messages to relieved readers across the State of Maine.

"THE PAINTER" KILLED BY POLICE DETECTIVE

An unidentified man, believed to be the multiple killer known as 'The Painter,' was shot and killed early yesterday morning in Auburn at the home of Andrew LaFleur. Believed to be responsible for the deaths of four students; Angela Carrington, Carrie Mortonsen, Deanna Porter and Randy Kingston, over the past several weeks, The Painter had been the subject of the largest manhunt in State of Maine history.

The man, who carried no form of identification, was shot to death by Maine State Police Detective Jake Lewis shortly after 1:00 am at 12 Martindale Road in Auburn. Sergeant Reed Sanderson, who was also involved in the sting operation, was disguised as local resident Andrew LaFleur and was attacked when he drove LaFleur's car into his driveway.

The man, believed to be The Painter, attacked Sanderson with a knife inflicting several wounds to the chest and arm of the MSP Detective before Lewis arrived and, according to police reports, fired two Smith & Wesson 45 caliber rounds into the alleged mass murderer. The first shot, according to Lewis, hit the assailant in the neck knocking him to the ground while the second, to the man's chest, proved to be fatal. "I had to act quickly because my partner was bleeding badly and was being held at knife point by the killer," said Lewis in a brief statement. "I would very much like to have kept him alive but when he reached for the knife I had no choice but to shoot to kill."

The death was the result of a sting operation put in place last week when State law enforcement officials learned that LaFleur, 23, son of Wallace LaFleur and grandson of Henri LaFleur, well known local businessmen and philanthropists, may have been targeted as the next victim. There has been no word as to how or why this was determined.

According to the police report Sanderson drove LaFleur's car home after the young man had been at Gipper's, a local sports bar, and the assailant was waiting in the trees beside the driveway. The knife used in the attack on Sanderson is believed to be the same one used in the killing of at least two students.

The body of the assailant has been taken to the State Crime Lab in Augusta where an autopsy will be performed today. The hope is that the young man, appearing to be between 20-25 years, old can be identified based on fingerprints or dental records. If anyone has information relative to the assailant or the attack please contact the Maine State Police.

The State Police have determined that a duffel bag found at the scene of the attack belonged to the assailant but have not revealed its contents. There was no information on whether The Painter, so-called because he left messages in blood at the scene of the murders, was carrying any message.

Sanderson, 43, an eighteen-year veteran of the State Police and a member of the Criminal Investigation Division, is reported to be in stable condition at Central Maine Medical Center in Lewiston.

~ 70 ~

Reed was resting comfortably in Room 114 at Central Maine Medical Center when Scott, Amy and Sandy walked in.

Scott was the first to get to him and as he went to give his father a bear hug the nurse on duty interrupted his action by saying, "Whoa there. That's the side your Dad was injured on. If you want to hug him walk around to the other side."

Scott did as he was told and laid his head on his Dad's left shoulder after kissing his cheek.

"Hey, Buddy. How you dooin?" said Reed in his best Joey Tripiano imitation.

"Great Dad. How you doin?"

"Pretty good, I guess. A little sore but none the worse for the wear. Hey Sandy, Hi Darling."

Amy, who was holding a bouquet of mixed flowers bent over to kiss him and tears welled in her eyes. "Oh Reed. Look at your eye!"

"Shhh! We can't have any of that," Reed replied, taking his good arm and gently wrapping it around her neck to pull her closer. "I love you…. thanks for the flowers."

"I love you too," she whispered into his neck.

"The doctor says that the cuts were mostly superficial and besides the stitches it took to sew me up there is nothing serious. My eye looks worse than it really is. I'm told that I'll be able to go home tomorrow."

"I hope so," said Sandy. "There's a bunch of yard work to do and a lot of wood to split."

"Since when have we split wood?" asked Reed.

"With oil prices climbing I thought it would be a good time to start," said Sandy. "Besides, now that The Painter is gone, you're going to need a hobby."

"You know, I do have some time coming after all the hours we put in. Just maybe we ought to plan an ice fishing trip - what do you say, Scott?"

"That'd be great Dad. How soon can we go?"

"Whoa Scotty, interjected Sandy. We've got to let your Dad get healthy before we go fishing. You remember how he plans on hauling tuna out of that lake. He's going to need his full strength."

"There's tuna in Moose Lake?" asked Amy innocently.

"Not really," replied Sandy. "But there's some magnificent tires."

~ 71 ~

Three days after the death of The Painter Lieutenant Bradbury called for a meeting in Gray of all personnel who had worked on that case. By the time that he arrived at 8:30 everyone else was already there milling about in the conference room where all of the extra chairs had been set up.

Bradbury made a point to speak with Reed, who had been released the night before and made a special effort to attend with the promise that he would return home immediately afterward. He also sought out Jake Lewis with whom he chatted briefly and then he called the gathering to order.

"If you will all please take a seat I will try to take as little time as possible," said Bradbury. He waited for a moment as the chairs filled and the room grew silent.

"First, on behalf of the MSP, the Division, and the people of Maine, I want to thank and congratulate all of you on your efforts to solve this incredibly demanding case of multiple murders. I am aware of just how much time, energy and sacrifice went into this case and I certainly realize how you went above and beyond the call of duty. Although we still have a great deal of paperwork left to do before we put this to bed, we will get through this as quickly as possible. I hope you then will have an opportunity to get the time off and take the vacations that many of you put on hold, and you so richly deserve.

"I am always leery," Bradbury continued, "to single out any individuals because solving crimes, especially complex ones like we had, are team efforts, but - yes, you knew a but was coming, I feel that I would be amiss to not have a special round of applause for Reed Sanderson and Jake Lewis who played major roles in helping rid our State of this particularly dangerous psychopath."

A rousing round of applause followed along with some "high fives" and good natured ribbing for both.

Bradbury assumed control. "Now, since we're all together,

there are many loose ends to be tied up and questions yet to be answered that I think should be discussed here. First, the identity of the individual killed by Jake in the line of duty remains a mystery. We had no success finding either a record of his finger prints or dental records. There are no records of either in our data base. We did run his blood type and found it to be AB negative which is not only very rare but also matches that which was found at the crime scene in Windham."

"So what you're saying," offered Wiz, "is that we know he is the killer but not who the killer is."

"That's right, Wiz," said Bradbury. "That's the way it appears. As many of you already know, we found a duffel bag that he brought with him to LaFleur's house the other night. In addition to plastic gloves, rope, duct tape and the knife that he used, there also was a brush and a note. Although the note was unlike the others that have been left in size or style, the handwriting did match the others."

"What did the note say?" asked Tom Lombardo.

"It was encrypted like all of the others but when deciphered said, 'Gratification is near.' The cipher, using the system that Wiz identified earlier, was every third letter."

"How can that be?" asked Joe Quinn. "We heard from Wayne Porter that there were five individuals involved in the rape of that dancer twenty some years ago and Andy LaFleur would have been the fifth victim. How could there have been two more?" His voice trailed off in a tone of confusion.

"I don't know, but at least we won't have to worry about that any more," answered Bradbury.

"Did you find anything else?" asked Quinn

"There was an empty beer bottle in the bag - Budweiser."

"He must have drank it in the van while sitting there waiting and watching his next victim," suggested Lombardo.

"You'd think so, but there was no alcohol in his blood. As you all know we found a white Dodge van parked a few hundred yards from where LaFleur lives. The killer had the key to it in his pocket. But, like the man himself, it provided no real clues. The interior was scrubbed clean, the VIN number had been filed indistinguishable, and the vehicle was not registered. There was one license plate on the back, that obviously had been stolen, thus keeping it from being reported to the NCIC.

"Wouldn't a stolen plate trigger an investigation?" asked Susan Weeks, sitting in on the briefing.

"No," answered Bradbury. "The National Crime Index Computer is only notified if a vehicle, or both plates are stolen. If he has stolen one plate from a white, like-model van of a similar year an officer could pull it up, see that it's not stolen, and therefore not call it in to the NCIC. He could have done this for years and avoided detection."

"So, what do we really know?" asked Quinn.

"We know that the man known as The Painter, the man responsible for the deaths of four young people, is dead. We don't know who he is, where he comes from or why he did it. We have a 1989 white Dodge van with no VIN, no registration, and no license plates. The lab boys dusted it for prints and found nothing. It appears that it had been sanitized - scrubbed from stem to stern. They're checking for fibers in the back but it appears our killer was a neat freak. I'd love to find out where he lived. I'll bet it's immaculate."

~ 72 ~

Reed placed the vase of fresh cut flowers in the center of the kitchen table, laid the silverware in the proper locations, took out the linen napkins from the drawer and folded them neatly in half before placing them on the table.

"You realize, Reed, it's Amy that's coming to dinner, not Martha Stewart," suggested Sandy as he dipped a wooden spoon into the spaghetti sauce simmering on the stove.

"I know, Sandy, but I want everything to be just right. The four of us don't get a chance to be together often, and besides, I'm not trying to convince Martha Stewart to move back in. You know though, Dad, she's about your age…so maybe …"

"Don't even think about it. I can't stand tofu, don't own a taffeta scarf, and never made Christmas ornaments out of popsicle sticks," chuckled Sandy.

Scott popped his head in through the kitchen door. "Can someone hand me a dirty towel?" I'm afraid Barney got a little muddy on his walk. Hey, I see we're having spaghetti. Can I check to see if it's done?"

"If Sandy says it's okay," said Reed, throwing him a towel.

Reed opened a bottle of Shiraz, Amy's favorite, to breathe, and began to re-fold the napkins when Sandy snapped. "You go change your clothes or put on some cologne or something while I make the salad. You're driving me crazy."

After wiping down the dog Scott removed a piece of spaghetti from the kettle with a plastic pasta utensil and laid it on the counter. He then picked it up in his fingers and pretended to be a pitcher, looking into the catcher for a sign. Sandy, seeing Scott's action, gingerly dropped into a crouch in front of the sink and placed one finger between his legs.

"Gimme the smoke, Scotty Boy. Let's send this Punch and Judy hitter back to El Paso."

A smile broke wide across the boy's face as he went into his windup and proceeded to purposely throw the string of spaghetti over Sandy's head where it stuck against the kitchen wall.

"Ya got 'em swinging Scott. He couldn't handle the heat up in the wheel house."

"Thanks, Sandy. I think the 'sketti's' done, too."

There was a weak knock on the door and Amy, wearing a pair of jeans and a light blue ribbed sweater, walked into the kitchen.

"Hi, Mom," said Scott, as he put his arms around his mother.

"Hi Amy," echoed Sandy.

"Hi Darling – hey, Sandy," responded Amy. "Boy it smells good in here."

"Thanks Amy, It's Old Spice," replied Sandy whistling the familiar commercial jingle.

"That's not what I meant Sandy, but I'm sure that smells good too."

Reed walked into the room and gingerly put his arms around Amy drawing her close to him. He leaned in for a deep kiss, thought better of it and gave her a warm hug nestling his head into the crook of her neck. "Hi, Baby," he whispered into her ear.

"Hi, Reed, How are you?"

"Better now," he replied. "How about a glass of wine? I have Shiraz – it's a brave little vintage… August, I think… and supper is just about ready. Sandy, care for some wine?"

"No, thanks anyway, but I think I'll spend a little quality time with a Newcastle Brown."

Reed poured two glasses of wine and was joined at the kitchen table by Amy and Scott while Sandy carried over the food. When everything was on the table Scott got up, grabbed a box of matches from a drawer and lit two long white candles before shutting off the kitchen light.

"My, isn't this cozy," said Amy.

"Just like the Waltons," said Sandy

"You're dating yourself Sandy," chuckled Amy.

"That's not all bad – some of the best dates I've ever had," retorted Sandy as everyone laughed.

The rest of the dinner was filled with easy laughter and warm conversation. As much as Reed wanted to be alone with Amy he recognized the need for quality time for all and spent the night basking in the camaraderie. Before anyone realized, it was ten o' clock and Sandy declared that he "needed his beauty sleep and was turning in."

"You may want to sleep right through tomorrow, Dad, if that's the reason you're going to bed."

"Good night Sandy. Thanks for everything," said Amy.

Scott gave Sandy a hug and then announced that he, too, was going to bed. As he walked down the hallway to his room, Barney trailing a couple of strides behind, he hollered back at his mother and asked, "Will you tuck me in after I brush my teeth?"

"Huh?" asked Reed

"Doesn't normally get tucked in, I gather," said Amy

"No, doesn't normally offer to brush his teeth," replied Reed.

"I'm surprised that he would want me to tuck him in. It's been awhile."

"You're never too old to be tucked in, Amy."

A couple of minutes later Scott hollered to his mother that he was ready and she went into his bedroom and sat down beside him on the bed.

"Mom, it is really great to have you here tonight."

"I have enjoyed it too, Scott."

He sat up so he could reach his arms around his mother. She held him tight pulling him close to her chest and gave him a kiss on the forehead. He then slid down as she stood and pulled the blankets up around his neck saying, "Get some sleep – I love you, Scott."

Afterward she returned to the living room to find Reed sitting on the couch with his stockinged feet up on the coffee table. He had taken out two brandy snifters and filled each half full with Grand Marnier. He handed her one as she sat down.

"Ahh, the good stuff," she said.

"Nothing is too good for you, Babe." He smiled softly as he took her hand in his and looked deeply into her eyes. "It's good to have you here, Amy. The house just isn't the same without you being here."

"It feels good, Reed. It's good to see Sandy and I miss the daily inter-actions with Scott. I know you're doing what you feel is right but I just can't stand to be hurt again. I'm sorry"

He leaned his head into the crook of her neck and closed his eyes. It wasn't what he wanted to hear but for this moment it just felt right.

~ 73 ~

Jake knew exactly what he needed to do. He had begun his task last week and although he hadn't had any success he felt he was onto something and was headed in the right direction. Jake was situated in the Bowdoin College Library looking through twenty-five year old microfilm from the Times Record, a daily paper serving the Mid-coast region of Maine.

It stands to reason, he thought to himself, that if the events were as Wayne Porter described them, the woman would have gone to the police to report the rape and perhaps there was some mention in the paper under Police Log.

Last week, Jake had spent one entire morning looking for such an article covering March of 1984 and today he had progressed into April. The first two weeks revealed nothing, but finally, in the April 20th edition, there appeared a box listing crimes reported to the Brunswick Police for that week. In the list was: Vicky Chimes, 23, of 117 Chamberlain Ave. reported that she was raped by five men on the evening of April 17th.

Great, he thought, now that he had an actual date he could stop at the police department and see what kind of archival system they have. In fact, perhaps before I do that, I should call Tim Stockwell and ask him. It might save me some time. Jake looked on his cell phone for Tim's number and then, while walking away from the other people on his floor, punched it in. His call was picked up on the second ring.

"Hello," came the response.

"Hello, Tim. Jake Lewis. How's it goin? How's the Missus?'"

"Everything's great, Jake - hey, congratulations on solving that case with The Painter. How's Reed doing?"

"Pretty well, Tim. Say that's the case I'm trying to wrap up. Do you keep archival records at the department?"

"Sure do - in the basement. We go back to about 1980, I believe. What do you need?"

"I'm investigating a rape charge in 1984, said Jake. The fathers of the students killed by The Painter plus Wallace LaFleur were supposedly involved in a rape in April of that month. I want to follow up on what happened to that charge and what was the real name of the woman making the complaint."

"Listen," said Tim. "Why don't I help you. I'm at the station now. Where are you?"

"I'm at the Bowdoin library. I've been studying micro-film."

"Good. Come on down. I'll take a look and maybe I can save you some time."

"Thanks, Tim. Check on a report dated April 18, 1984."

"Will do - see you when you get here."

The Brunswick Police Department is located on Federal Street, just a short drive from where Jake was located. He made the quick trip and after saying hello to the information officer on duty headed downstairs where he found Tim poring over pages in a box titled APRIL - 1984. After the two men shook hands Tim gave Jake some disappointing news. "Jake, I don't know why, because the info on either side is available, but the Daily Activity Log you are looking for is missing."

~ 74 ~

Andy LaFleur was not, by definition, a *bon vivant*. Nevertheless, he had no shortage of female company, had plenty of discretionary income, and enjoyed many of the finer things in life.

On this evening he chose to dine at Mac's Steak House, one of the areas finest, known for their variety of distinctive rubs and acclaimed cuts of top grade beef. A meal at Mac's is not to be rushed and when accompanied by a bottle of fine wine and meaningful companionship it can be enjoyable, indeed.

Tonight Andy was dining with a young lady who worked as a secretary at his family's business. He was advised against such action but those who were doing the advising had not looked into Cierra Larson's eyes, run their fingers over her satin skin or been enveloped by her arms and mouth in a passionate kiss. With her honey-blonde, shoulder-length hair and trim figure she was truly an attractive young lady or, as Andy was wont to say, 'I've seen more beautiful women, I just can't remember when."

He was three years her senior but found her to be witty, warm and charming. Together their conversation bounded across the barriers of age, element and experience and often was interspersed with laughter.

This was only their second date but as he sat across from her sipping a glass of Barbaresco from the Piemonte region of Northern Italy he knew it wouldn't be the last.

"Can I freshen your glass?" he asked, picking up the bottle wrapped in a white creased linen napkin.

"I really shouldn't. It's delicious Andy", said Cierra putting both hands around her glass, looking straight into his eyes, "but I have to get up early tomorrow and must have a clear head."

"Sounds like you've got yourself an employment issue. Should I look into it for you?"

"Thanks anyway. Not only do I like my job, but I like my boss."

"Just say the word and I'll have you transferred into my department."

"I don't think that would be wise. Especially if we are going to continue seeing each other."

"Well, I certainly hope that I can see a lot more of you."

Her laughter interrupted him, causing him to go back over his words.

"You know what I mean. I'd like us to go out again is what I meant."

"I know what you meant. I'd like that, too but I really need to get going now if you don't mind."

Andy paid the bill, left a handsome tip for the waitress and drove Cierra to her home where she lived with both of her parents and her younger brother. He walked her to the door and waited for her to make the first move. When she leaned into him, leading with her full lips, he placed both arms around her and matched the passion of her kiss with his own.

"Andy, is there anything you don't do well?" she said looking through his eyes, absorbing his kiss.

"I don't say good night particularly well," Andy replied - "when it's something that I don't want to do."

With that he gave her one last kiss raising his left hand behind her head and pulling her close. She allowed herself to be molded into his embrace and responded by placing her right hand on his cheek, rubbing softly. Reluctantly he walked away waving as he entered his car.

While driving his RX7 the few miles home his mind raced and heart pounded. Despite having so many attractive young women to choose from he was convinced that Cierra was the *special* one he had searched for.

Pulling into his driveway he thought of when, where, and what his next date should be with her. Andy felt a real connection with Cierra and he was determined to make their next date something different, something defining. As he shut his car door it was understandable that his mind was on the beautiful young woman.

It was too bad because he did not see the young man with the knife step between the blue spruces until it was much too late.

~ 75 ~

Reed and Jake looked down at the body of Andy LaFleur laying on his back in his driveway, his neck cut from ear to ear. "I was afraid of this," offered Jake. "I really felt we might have a copycat killer."

"What made you think such a thing might happen?" asked Reed.

"Well, we know The Painter is dead and with all the publicity inherent in this case everyone knew that Andy LaFleur was The Painter's next target and that slitting the throat was the chosen methodology of the killer. With all the weirdos in today's society I was afraid that the coverage in the local papers might spawn some thrill seeker trying to take advantage of the publicity."

Reed looked down at the grisly scene. "Just what we needed."

Yellow crime tape surrounded the property but could not keep out the legions of law enforcement personnel representing several jurisdictions. Because of the obvious degree of renewed notoriety in the case there were also dozens of reporters, camera men and passersby, all of whom wanted to get closer.

Reed saw Wallace LaFleur storming toward him and braced himself for the storm. "I thought you said you were putting a surveillance team on him?"

"With the death of The Painter we didn't think it was necessary," replied Reed, "and I thought you weren't concerned with the inherent danger?" he countered.

"There is no reason for his death," snarled LaFleur. "It never should have happened."

"I'm very sorry Mr. LaFleur, said Reed changing his tone as he saw tears well up in the man's eyes. I didn't know your son, other than our brief act of subterfuge but he seemed like a fine young man and I have heard nothing but good things about him."

LaFleur did not respond to Reed's remarks but instead walked away muttering "the fucking bitch." Reporters and news anchors rushed toward him as he prepared to depart the property but he marched by and through them refusing to acknowledge their existence.

Several feet from where lay LaFleur's body Jake noticed a series of scuff marks in the gravel driveway along with the beginning of a trail of dark drops. "I wonder," said Jake kneeling down. "It appears that they may have scuffled before Andy died. These appear to be drops of blood."

"Don't touch it Jake," said Steve Mangino, gathering evidence for the ERT.

"No problem, Steve. This ain't my first rodeo, you know. Get us the blood types on this stuff as soon as possible, will you."

~ 76 ~

Reed was up earlier than normal on this seasonably warm morning. Because of his bandages he was still unable to shower but he could use the tub if the water was not too high. Sandy, of course, was only too willing to help.

"Here, I'll do your back," he said with a face cloth full of soap. "Do you want a rubber ducky?"

"What I want is for you to do what you have to and then get gone."

Between the two of them they were able to reach all of the significant locations and Sandy reveled in washing and shampooing Reed's hair. "I feel like I'm working with Barbara Bush as white as it is," Sandy said. "It's nice to know I'll have something to fall back on when I get old."

"You're already old," replied Reed.

"Age is a relative thing, my boy."

With an air of finality Reed replied, "Exactly, you're an aged relative."

After what seemed like a lengthy time Reed completed his morning ablutions and said good bye to all of the family including Barney. As he was driving toward the barracks in Gray his phone rang. Nestled in a car holder he pushed the button to activate the call and heard the voice of Frank Wolcott, one of the technicians from the State Crime Lab on the other end.

"Hello, Reed, …Frank Wolcott"

"Yea, hi, Frank. How are things in Augusta?"

"I'm busier 'n a one-armed paper-hanger but I do have some information for you from the LaFleur crime scene."

"Great, Frank … Whatta ya got?"

"First, you and Jake asked Steve Mangino about some dark splattered spots and you were right, that was blood, and not from LaFleur. Those drops are from a very rare type AB-negative."

That can't be, thought Reed - *that's the same as The Painter,* and then out loud; "Were those drops fresh or could they have been from last week when The Painter was shot?"

"They were fresh, Reed, clearly not a week old - and according to Steve they weren't found in the same location, anyway."

"I knew that but I had to ask," said Reed. "It's just too much of a coincidence to have both a killer and a copycat with type AB negative blood when it's found in just one percent of the population. Anything else?"

"Yes, LaFleur was found lying on his back and the ME did not do a thorough exam before he was bagged and sent up here for an autop..."

"What are you getting at?" Reed interrupted.

"Well the boy, er ... young man, was pretty badly torn up in his anus. It seems that whoever cut his throat took an object to his anus and bludgeoned him pretty badly. From the exam it was some type of blunt object possibly a bottle that was used in the attack, post mortem, and in his anal cavity there was a note."

"What can you tell me about the note?"

"There were no prints, which has been the MO on all the other messages that we've looked at and it was in a totally different cursive handwriting. It was done on plain white paper using LaFleur's blood type, probably during the commission of the crime. We will have a handwriting expert take a look at it as soon as possible."

"Good ... what else?"

"Well, it was not encrypted Reed. It simply said, "He loves it. He can't get enough of it.""

~ 77 ~

Reed's chest and arm ached after another long day and he knew that it would only get better with three more Advil or a trip to Jimmy D's place for a cheeseburger and a libation. It did not take a great deal of persuasion to convince Jake to meet him there.

Reed was sitting in the parking lot just finishing up a call, saying good night to Scott when Jake pulled up beside him. They entered the intimate establishment together and were immediately recognized by regulars.

"Wazzup guys."

"Hi Jake, hey Reed, wanna go bowling?"

Sitting at the bar was a couple of retired regulars who resembled Mutt and Jeff of cartoon fame, playing cribbage. Denny, the short one who was quick to needle his immense companion and then respond with a cackle, was saying, "For Christ sake R.T. will you please play. I'm down two dollars and thirty eight cents and I've only got two weeks off."

Putting down a sports magazine R.T. responded, "Oh Wow," in a deep voice and tone as dry as a popcorn fart. "I didn't know it was my turn. I'm doin' my research on the Rice Owls this week."

The detectives greeted both of them and were headed toward the back booth when the owner and bar's namesake walked out of the kitchen with his small white towel over one shoulder and cheeseburger plate in one hand.

"Hey boys," he quickly offered.

"Hi, Jim," said Reed

"Say Hey, Jimmy D. What's shakin'? Jake responded"

"James Bond's drinks, most of Indonesia after that last earthquake and hopefully my wife's ass when I get home tonight," answered Jimmy D with a smile. "I'll be right back to get your orders."

Reed and Jake settled into their favorite booth, ordered two beers and a plate of Nacho Grande and engaged in conversation relative to the case that had consumed so much of their time.

"Are we getting any closer to solving this thing, Reed?"

"You know Jake, sometimes I wonder. There's something we're missing. Let's see if we can't break this down a bit." Taking out a note pad of lined paper and a Cross pen he made two headings at the top of the page.

WHAT WE DO KNOW

There is another murderer
A woman was reportedly raped
The Painter is dead
The message found on LaFleur was the same as was reported to have been said to the woman years ago.
The last note was written in a different handwriting
All of the murders were committed using a knife
A van was found at the scene of The Painter's death

WHAT WE DON'T KNOW

Who the second murderer is
Who are the intended 6th and 7th victims
What blood type the murderer has
Why did the rape case not go to trial
Where is the case file
Who is the woman, where does she live, and how has she been able to avoid recognition
Who killed Andy LaFleur
Who wrote the most recent note
Who does the white van belong to
How did the "new" killer get to LaFleur's home
Why, when, and where will the killer strike again

"You know Reed, said Jake looking at the list, "there are a lot of valid points here but the last question is the one that really needs answering."

Jake took a long draft from his glass and then wiped his mouth with the back of his hand. "If we are going to believe Wayne Porter, then there were five men present at the rape scene and now all five men have lost a child at the hand of some killer or killers. Porter said that when they got done raping this girl named Vicki, Wally LaFleur used a beer bottle on her. Don't forget that The Painter had a beer bottle with him when he was shot and killed yet no alcohol was found in his system. The correlation seems obvious that what was done to Vicki is the same as what was done to LaFleur by our unknown killer and it is probable that it was also going to be done by The Painter." Jake continued, "so doesn't it stand to reason that the new killer and The Painter have some connection or knowledge of one another?"

Reed thought for a minute and then spoke. "Jake I've got something I want to bounce off of you. Let's assume for a minute that this woman, who gets raped in 1984, gets pregnant through that attack. If she was raped in mid-April then she would have given birth in or around mid-January, 1985. That would mean that her child would be in his early twenties. Could The Painter have been her son? He looked to be about that old."

Jake continued the explanation that Reed had begun. "Then he gets killed, before they finish with their plan, or we find out who he is, so she kills the next victim and, according to her messages, will kill the next two, whoever they are."

Reed responded, "you're right. We need to find out who the mystery woman is who gave birth in a Brunswick hospital around mid-January, 1985 and ask her some questions."

"I find it fascinating, too," Jake replied, "that the one file we're hunting for, the one that has the information on the report of the rape, is the one that is missing. I'm going to continue pursuing that. There was an old-timer named Kelly who retired from the Brunswick PD about five years ago. I'm going to give him a call. Ya' know, Reed, if we kiss enough frogs we're bound to find a prince."

~ 78 ~

It took Jake three phone calls to get hold of Jackson Kelly, a retired cop in his early seventies, who had served almost forty years as a member of the Brunswick Police Department.

He had twice been offered the position of Chief but both times had declined, preferring his role as Detective working as a Patrol Commander. He had since retired and spent much of his time on Bailey's Island where he lived in a renovated camp on the water with his wife and English Spaniel.

Years ago he and Jake had worked on a case involving a series of burglaries in Brunswick and had bumped into one another several other times over the years. Because he was a bit hard of hearing, Jake had to identify himself three times on the phone before it registered with Kelly.

"Oh…Jake, …yes, Jake Lewis .. How are you, Jake?"

"I'm fine Jackson. How's retirement treating you?"

"Not bad, Jake. I grow some vegetables, play golf twice a week when the weather's good and take Carol shopping every Friday morning, so I can't complain. Wouldn't do any good anyway, now would it," he chuckled.

"Don't believe it would Jackson."

"So what's up Jake. You didn't call me up to talk about my garden."

"You're right, Jackson. I'm stuck on a case and was hoping you could help me. A couple of dozen years ago there was a woman who went to the police in Brunswick claiming she'd been raped by five men. Nothing ever seemed to come from the complaint and the file containing the log has disappeared. Do you remember anything about the case?"

"It seems that I do, Jake…not the particulars but I remember being involved a little bit. It was a gang rape involving some college kids from Bowdoin, I believe. We always had to be so careful when it involved Bowdoin students."

"Why's that?"

"You know… high visibility. Usually rich kids from away who had parents in high places. Almost always related to drinking."

"You nailed it, Jackson."

"Yea, it's coming back to me some. I wasn't the primary on the case but I put in a little time on it - interviewed a couple of the kids and the girl."

"Jackson did you, by chance, keep your own log of the cases that you worked on?"

"Why of course, Jake, we all did. It wasn't official or nothing, but we kept our own notes"

"… and is that something you would still have? Or was that all thrown away when you retired?"

"What kind of cop do you think I am, Jake? I have all my stuff in boxes in my house in Brunswick."

"You're the best, Jackson. Do you think I could meet you at the house and help you go through it?" asked Jake, his voice rising with excitement.

"You're welcome to meet me there, Jake, but I really won't need your help finding it. I kept everything in order by years - in case I was called to be an expert witness or something. I'll meet you at 2 Davis Street tomorrow, over behind the Bowdoin pines. Let's say 8:00 am, I don't get up as early as I used to."

"That will be great. Thanks, Jackson."

"No, Thank you, Jake. I miss being a cop."

~ 79 ~

Jake arrived promptly at 8:00 am and found Jackson Kelly was already in his home. He rang the bell and then, because he knew the older man was hard of hearing, stepped into the pantry off the kitchen.

As Jake looked around, walking into the small, musty kitchen he could hear Kelly puttering in the basement. Jake advanced to an open door in the kitchen and hollered down, "Jackson, it's Jake. I let myself in."

The retired cop started up the stairs, each step a challenge due to a recent knee replacement. In his arms was a brown, cardboard box the type that was designed to look like a filing box with one white end and lines for writing in the subject matter and year.

"Glad ya' did. I never would have heard you," he replied. "How are ya' Jake. It's been a little while but you don't look no worse for the wear."

"Doing good, Jackson, but this case is driving us crazy. I hope you can help us."

"Well, let's see," Jackson replied, putting the box down on the kitchen table and readjusting his thick glasses. "What was the date you wanted checked?"

"The rape supposedly occurred on April 17, 1984, was reported on the 18th, and appeared in the Times Record in the April 20 edition. What do you have about that time, Jackson?"

Only the top of Kelly's head was visible to Jake, mostly balding with thin white wisps above both ears. The rest of his face was buried in the box meticulously examining his own hand-written and designed filing system. Finally he rose, like a bear with a stream salmon, and said, "Here it is - this is what I was looking for."

Jake watched as he took a thin, brown, dog-eared spiral notebook out of the box with hand writing throughout. "Looks like quite an intricate system of note-taking," said Jake sarcastically.

"Aw hell," said Kelly, "today everything is filed electronically thanks to the Freedom of Information Act, but 'back in the day' we all had our own systems and kept our own notes."

Kelly continued, "I remember hearing one day about a guy over in North Yarmouth who was found playing with himself in a barn. The lady who found him said, 'You shouldn't be doing that.' Now the guy wasn't real sound of mind but when he heard what she said he looked up at her and said, 'Why? Mine, ain't it?'

Jake chuckled out loud as Kelly pointed out the analogy. "See, that's how I feel about my notes. They might not be as flashy as some but they're mine - and they always worked just fine, thank you."

"What do you have relative to that rape case?" Jake asked.

With the glee that comes from a sense of purpose Kelly turned to the requisite date and said, "Here it is - April 18, 1984. I was asked to interview two of the five people charged with the crime as well as the victim.

"The girl who filed the complaint was listed as Vicki Chimes of Chamberlain Avenue. I don't believe that was her real name but it's all she gave. It says here that she didn't know the name of the men involved but she reported the address and it was traced back to Charlie Carrington. T'was a bit embarrassing, as I recall, because it was the in-laws place and they knew nothing about it. Charlie denied having anything to do with it and when it didn't go to trial I guess everything was forgotten."

"I was asked to interview him and a Wayne Porter. They both downplayed the whole thing saying 'the girl was making something out of nothing.'"

"The girl admitted to being a dancer but insisted she was not a prostitute and was forced to not only have sex with the five of them, but was sexually assaulted as well. It says here that her blood/alcohol level, was well above the legal limit of intoxication."

"Who interviewed the other three?" asked Jake.

"Let's see, it says that Pokey Martin interviewed Blake Kingston and Ben Mortonsen. His real name was Luther but everyone called him Pokey, cause he was so slow," Kelly offered. "He retired years ago... probably raising turtles," said the old man who chuckled at his own joke.

"And let's see, the last person that was named in the assault was Wallace LaFleur and he was interviewed by the primary on the case - Tim Stockwell."

~ 80 ~

"Tim Stockwell was the primary detective on this case?" repeated Jake with the tone of a teenaged parent being told that their child was studying at the library. "And he interviewed Wallace LaFleur?"

"Yup. That's what I have written here. I've got a bunch of notes from Pokey on his questioning but it don't appear that I got anything on LaFleur."

"Anything else you got?" Jake asked

"Says the info all went to Mike Pioretti, the District Attorney, who was the Assistant DA at the time, but it was never brought to trial. According to my notes from the primary there just wasn't enough substantial evidence to take it to trial. I guess both Stockwell and Pioretti agreed on that."

"I believe that Stockwell also interviewed the girl and the final report that we got back was that she was just some floozy dancer trying to make a quick buck off some Bowdoin College guys."

"Boy, this just doesn't ring true to me, Jackson. Does it to you?"

"Seemed kinda quick, Jake. I remember thinking that at the time but I did what I was told - interview them two boys and the girl and give my report to the primary."

"One other thing I wrote on the corner of my sheet - I musta heard this later and just doodled it on the cover page and that was that. The girl visited some nurse over at the air station - don't know what that means and don't know if any of this will help - but don't forget, Jake. It's mine ain't it?" Kelly's chuckle filled the room.

Jake thanked the man profusely and headed out of the small home two steps at a time. He rammed his transmission into drive and sent gravel flying as he headed out of the driveway.

Why, he thought, *wouldn't Tim Stockwell tell me that he was the primary on the case and not only oversaw the investigation, but brought it to the assistant district attorney with a recommendation that it wasn't a strong enough case to go forward. Surely it couldn't be that he forgot. Why is he holding back information? Why guess, Jake concluded , when I can go to the source.*

Tim Stockwell was not in when Jake stopped at the Brunswick PD and inquired. No one was sure just where he was, he hadn't been seen since the day before. Jake got his home number from dispatch and tried both that and his cell phone but had no success in reaching him on either number, leaving messages on both.

I'm starting to feel like Alice in Wonderland, thought Jake, *because this case is getting curiouser and curiouser.*

~ 81 ~

Since 1951, Brunswick Naval Air Station has played a major role in the socio-economic makeup of the town and region. Comprised of 3,300 acres, or almost 12% of the town's land mass, it has provided employment for almost 5,500 individuals, both military and civilian, and will have been responsible for $140 million of community income when it closes in 2011. BNAS maintains a medical clinic as part of the support provided for staffing and nearby citizenry.

Jake decided that if Jackson had made an annotated note, no matter how small, concerning a possible visit by the mystery woman, then he should make a trip over there.

Driving onto the base was much simpler than in the past. By showing his Maine State Police badge he was granted access and given directions to the medical center. This was a small building with limited medical equipment and designed today for menial tasks prior to being sent to one of the town's two hospitals where greater care could be given.

The clinic was being staffed by a civilian who took care of the necessary paper work and a middle-aged military nurse. Jake walked in, spoke with the former and asked to see the latter.

A rather doughty older woman with short hair and thin frame hidden by a tan uniform and name tag reading "Jones," welcomed him into her office.

"Good morning, ma'am, Jake Lewis, Detective with the State Police. Lieutenant Jones, I believe?"

"Yes, good morning, Detective. How may I help you?"

"I'm working on a murder case and trying to find out the name and whereabouts of a woman who gave birth to a boy in early 1985."

"Is this related to the case of the students who were murdered, Detective?" she asked, while rearranging her glasses which had slipped down her nose.

"Yes, ma'am. But why would you surmise that?"

"It's all anybody around here is talking about since that Bowdoin girl was killed. It's disgusting, … but I don't know what brings you here."

"Do you mind if I ask you how long you've served in this capacity?"

"I've been at BNAS since 1979. At one point there was a staff of four but we have been downsized with the announcement of the base closing."

"Do you, or have you ever, dealt with child birth here on base?"

"No, when a woman comes in we determine if she's pregnant and then we discuss her options relative to the different hospitals, obstetric and gynecological specialists, and see that she gets the care she requires."

"Well, Lieutenant Jones, the woman we are investigating goes back to the spring of 1984 with an expected birth in January or early February, 1985. Might you remember if such a person came here for help. The reason that I ask is that a retired Brunswick cop made a note in his notebook stating that this woman went to BNAS for help."

Lieutenant Jones removed her glasses and put one end of the frame in her mouth. "Detective Lewis, how would you expect me to remember this particular woman?"

"She claimed that she was raped by five Bowdoin College students. She reported it to the police who did nothing with it. We have reason to believe that she may have been impregnated in this attack."

"Detective, now that you mention that, I do remember. She came in sometime in the fall. She was several months pregnant and was distraught. I tried to guide her to several physicians that we had used but she would have none of it. She refused to go to a hospital and even talked about getting an abortion. I assured her that that was not possible since she was in her second trimester. She was distressed and, quite frankly, I was afraid that she could have been suicidal."

"So, what did you do?"

"I did what I felt I had to do in the circumstances - what was best for her and her baby. I gave her the name of a mid-wife; a woman who was not opposed to going to a home to help with the delivery. Flipping through her rolodex and then grabbing a notepad she wrote down the name of a woman along with an address and a phone number. Hopefully this will be of some value to you Detective. Perhaps it will help you solve your case."

"I sure hope it does, Lieutenant, but somehow I think the mystery is just beginning to unravel Thanks for your help."

~ 82 ~

It did not take Jake long to call Reed and catch him up to speed on what he had just learned from Lieutenant Jones. Armed with the name and address of the midwife the two Detectives agreed to meet and then set off toward her home in Bristol.

The midwife lived on Pemaquid Point road just a short distance from one of Maine's most historic light houses. Her home was more of a camp than a home in size but the view of the rockbound coast from her front yard was spectacular. When Reed and Jake arrived she was sitting in a rocking chair in her living room knitting. A fire blazed in the fireplace behind her.

Sheila Crockett looked very much like one would imagine a midwife might look like if playing the part in a movie. She had long, white, yarn-like hair tied back behind her head, wore horn rim glasses and a blouse buttoned tight at the neck. Her long flowing wool skirt ended well below her knees.

She reminded Reed of Granny Clampett in The Beverly Hillbillies but she proved to be much less irascible. In fact, she was very helpful and had a clear mind with an accurate memory."I'm glad to meet you both," she said with a wan smile. "I get so few visitors now it's good to see some new faces."

Reed began, "Sheila, thanks for agreeing to meet with us. We understand that you are a midwife. How long have you served in that capacity?"

"Actually, I no longer practice midwifery. The laws are so much more complicated and demanding now. It used to be that we could go to a girl's house, deliver the baby, and if needed provide after care without the assistance of a physician, hospital, or so-called 'specialist.'"

"Today there is so much red tape and federal bureaucracy that it's just not worth it."

After listening to the lament of "the good ole days," Jake got to the purpose of their visit. "It's about the service that you provided that brings us here. We are feverishly looking for a woman who gave birth nine months after allegedly being raped by five Bowdoin College students."

"A retired cop remembered that this girl saw someone at BNAS and Lieutenant Jones remembered giving her your name. She was several months pregnant and wanted no part of doctors and hospitals. It was back in 1984-85."

The lady gently rubbed her chin with her left hand but responded quickly. "Ah, yes, I remember. She was already six months pregnant and said she didn't want the baby. I assured her that it was too late for any talk of abortion but that I could provide her with pre and post natal care and I could deliver her baby. She accepted my offer."

"Where was she living at the time?" Reed asked.

"She was living in an apartment, small but clean, over towards Bowdoin somewhere I believe."

"Do you remember her name?"

"Vicky Chimes. I'm sure it was not her real name but I didn't care. I remember the name because there was a three-masted schooner that has sailed up and down the coast for years named the *Victory Chimes*. So beautiful they put her on the back of the Maine quarter when it was minted in 2003. I'm pretty sure it still sails out of Rockland."

The men marveled at the clarity of her memory and were enthused when they asked her if she remembered the baby being born.

"Oh, yes, she replied. I remember the date very well. It was January 1st - New Year's Day, 1985. But gentlemen, she said with a pause - it wasn't a baby - it was babies."

~ 83 ~

"Excuse me?" said Reed, his voice expressing disbelief.

"Sonovabitch," said Jake succinctly, and then continued, "you're telling me that this mystery woman, who none of us know, had twins."

"Exactly," came the reply.

"Were they both boys?" asked Reed quickly.

"Absolutely. Two healthy baby boys."

"Did she, by any chance, have names for these boys?" Jake inquired.

"Not that I know of. I didn't ask her but I never heard her call them anything."

Reed stood and after taking a couple of steps closer to the fire asked, "But wouldn't she have to name them. Didn't she have to put her real name down on the birth information that you sent to the town office?"

"Normally yes," she replied, looking out of her living room window, but she begged me not to submit any paperwork. She said she had been gang raped, had no idea who the father was, and did not want to give anybody the satisfaction of having it recorded."

"I told her that I could lose my license but she pleaded with me and, because of her extenuating circumstances, I relented. Fact is, I felt downright sorry for her."

"Was she happy once the babies were born?" Jake asked.

"That's just it," the midwife replied, "she didn't want anything to do with those babies. She refused to breast feed them, didn't show any inclination to want to hold them, and disliked changing them. I visited her each day for a couple of weeks to make sure she was doing alright by them but then, one day, I showed up and was told by a girl in the next apartment that they had moved out. I never knew where. I never saw or heard from her again, but I kept my promise to her and until today never had a reason to talk about her. She never paid me but I didn't really expect her to."

"Was there anybody that came to visit her or called her while you were there - any relatives or friends?"

"Nope, nope and nope. I do believe that this girl was all alone. She was alone, frightened and angry - a dangerous combination."

"You're telling me," answered Reed.

~ 84 ~

After a few more minutes of conversation the detectives thanked the woman for her assistance and left after leaving her a card in case she thought of anything else of importance.

Reed and Jake met in Sheila Crockett's parking lot for a moment as much to marvel at the scenery as to clear their heads and compare notes prior to heading off for home. "I guess we can stop trying to get information from the local hospitals," said Jake. "It sounds like she never set foot in a hospital."

"You're right. And we now know who killed Andy LaFleur and how the blood found on the scene was the same rare type - identical twins equals identical DNA. Which means that we still have a deadly killer on the streets of Maine and we have no idea who he is or where he lives."

"What's the next step, partner?" asked Jake.

"I think we need to get the rest of the unit together to share the information that we have just learned and to plan a course of action. What do you think?"

"I think that Tim Stockwell has some questions to answer. I still haven't heard from him even though I left messages at work, at home, and on his cell phone. I find that pretty strange."

After a bit more small talk the two detectives headed back to Brunswick where they had left Reed's car. A few minutes later Jake was driving toward the barracks in Gray when his cell phone rang. Lifting it to his ear he heard, "Hello,… Detective. This is Kay Stockwell…. You left a message on our home phone for my husband."

"Hi Kay, Yes I did. Is he home?"

"No, and that's why I'm calling, Detective. This is just not like him. He's been missing for three days now and that is just not him. He hasn't been home, shown up at work and hasn't even called. I'm scared to death."

"When was the last time you saw him, Kay?"

"Three days ago. He came home from work, drank a beer, read the mail and then within a few minutes he was gone. He kissed me, told me that he loved me and then left. He didn't say where he was going or when he'd be home. He just got in his cruiser and drove off."

"You said he read the mail. Did you happen to see what was in the mail?"

"Three or four bills. Typical stuff from CMP, car payment… you know, and there was one letter addressed to him."

"Did you see who it was from?"

"No, I wondered when I saw it but there was no return address."

"Do you know what the letter said, was it typed?" asked Jake.

"No, I didn't get a good look at it but when I handed him a beer I saw that it was handwritten - printed, actually."

"Now Kay, think carefully. What did he do with the letter after he was done reading it?"

"He put it back in the envelope and jammed it in his pants pocket. I could tell he was upset and I even asked him if there was anything wrong but he said, no, and then kissed me and left."

"I'm sorry to have to ask this but, have you been having any difficulties … you know, with your marriage? Is it possible that he might be seeing someone else, or perhaps having money problems that have been weighing heavily on him?"

"No. Nothing like that. We have been married for almost twelve years, the second marriage for both of us, and have been getting along great, just like we always do. We may not be well off but we have enough money for what we want or need. He's been looking ahead to retiring sometime soon and we've been talking about where to go."

"Do you have any children?"

"We both have one from our previous marriages. My son Ralph, sells automobiles in Wiscasset and Tim has a daughter named Zulma who he won't talk about. He told me that she ran away from home when she was seventeen."

"Zulma?"

"Yes, Zulma. Old family name, I guess."

"He says he hasn't seen or spoken to her since. After that I guess he had an ugly divorce and his ex-wife moved down South somewhere."

"Has he received any other of these letters, or perhaps any strange phone calls recently - anything else that has alarmed him?"

"No. Nothing that I've seen or know about. Oh, I am so worried. What should I do?"

"I don't really know what to tell you. I'm sure he is fine and will be home soon. He's a good police officer and is probably just working on a case and didn't want to alarm you. But, Kay, if he does call in will you please be sure to have him call me immediately. I want to help him."

~ **85** ~

'The Voice' opened the cellar door and walked stealthily down the decrepit stairs. She reached the bottom and continued straight down the long musty corridor stopping momentarily to look at the cubicle on the left with a worn mattress, small television on an orange crate and metal bowl.

She passed several empty rooms until she arrived at one on the right that was locked. When she reached up to remove the key from the hook outside the door the individual inside stood, his gaunt body nearly naked and shivering, a dark hood placed around his neck, covering his head.

Unbuttoning her blouse, she walked inside. "Poor baby," she began. "You look cold. Can Mommy make my little man feel better?"

She reached inside his underwear and grasped his penis feeling it grow as she steadily slid her hand up and down the shaft. The young man said nothing as he knew better than to speak.

When he was totally erect, his penis pointing slightly upward, she took his hands and brought them up to her bare breasts. At first he simply cupped them but with her urging he began to rub and stroke the flesh, squeezing the nipples gently.

She then slid his hood slightly upward and pulled his head forward so that he could take her nipples into his mouth. His penis, hard and throbbing, was forced against his abdomen.

"You like that, don't you?" she cooed. "Just like when you were a baby. You always wanted to suck on my nipples but I couldn't stand having them played with. My beautiful breasts got so fat and droopy. It was disgusting. Men are so predictable. Put a pair of tits in front of them and they fawn all over them."

After a couple of minutes of allowing him to alternate his sucking and nibbling between breasts she stepped back and once again reached between his legs. She rubbed one testicle and then the other gently squeezing his scrotal sack.

"My little baby has grown up to be a man - nice and big and hard. Would my little man like Mommy to take care of this?" she asked, grabbing his manhood.

"Yes …please," he answered.

She slid her blouse off as he stood patiently waiting.

"Come here my little man."

The young man stood stone still as his mother continued to stroke him and after a short time he felt himself release. His mother picked her blouse up off the dirt floor and stared straight into his eyes. As she buttoned her blouse she spat venomously, "I have told you many times that I am the only one to ever allow you to spill your seed. Do you understand?"

He followed with a muffled affirmation.

She continued speaking as she ran her right hand through her hair. "You deserved a reward today after the job you did recently. You have always been the chosen one, the better, the brighter of the two and you have proven that once again with the killing of Andrew LaFleur much like that of Carrie Mortonsen and Randy Kingston."

She thought how many times she had used similar praise with his brother and relied upon their competitive instincts and need for approval to spark their efforts and need for acceptance.

He, of course, did not know his brother was dead and she would use that to her advantage - to further stroke his ego and desire.

"I have decided to let you remove the last two obstacles in our path. You have earned such an opportunity," she continued, reaching out to take his flaccid penis in her hand.

"Remember, with risk comes reward."

~ 86 ~

Wallace LaFleur was used to getting his way. For as long as he could remember he was a "mover and a shaker" forcing those around him, or better said, under him, to move and shake.

With the loss of his son came avoid that he could not fill. His relationship with his wife was platonic and without pretense. Oh, there had been a brief period when there was a semblance of romance but since the birth of his son he had felt fulfilled and saw no reason to pretend to love her simply for public consumption. He would have divorced her but she realized her role and chose not to rock the boat. There had once been a time when she complained about playing 'second fiddle' but when he responded, "Sweetheart, you're lucky you are still in the band," she knew it was useless to resist and their marriage had become a charade.

With the birth of a son Wallace had not only a future business partner but an heir. The family name of LaFleur would continue. He had been so proud of what Andrew stood for and the way that he got along with people. He, himself, had no interest in being garrulous but he could see how others might find that engaging. His life, beside his business, was his son.

In addition to being lonely he felt vindictive and decided that he would take matters into his own hands. That bitch had no reason to take the life of his pride and joy. Hadn't he acquiesced to all her demands? He had paid her over a million dollars - $50,000 a year for over twenty years, as retribution. One little transgression years ago and he had paid for that many times over. And now this. A million fucking dollars. What more did she want. He had sent cash to a post office box every month and all she had to do was keep her mouth shut and leave him alone. But the bitch couldn't even do that.

He was parked in front of the Windham Post Office and had his Bushnell Surveillance binoculars focused on Box 48. He had no idea what her name was or even what she looked like. Hell, it had been twenty plus years since he and the boys had fun with her. All he knew is that he put a packet of hundred-dollar bills into a manila envelope addressed to Occupant, PO Box 48 Windham, Maine on the 15th of each month.

Well, that was going to end. He figured paying her off to keep him out of jail and out of the newspaper was one thing. Then, when all of the children of those who raped her started to be killed he figured Andrew was immune. Why would she kill him? Surely she wouldn't kill the golden goose or, more accurately, the son of the golden goose. Perhaps she felt she was untouchable because I don't know her name or address, thought Wallace. Well, fuck her. I'll sit here until the cows come home or until the bitch comes to empty the contents of Box 48.

He knew that the mail from Auburn to Windham would take just one day to deliver, and knew that the mail was put into the boxes in the morning, so he had arrived shortly after 10:00am and had parked in a spot a distance away. With the help of his 20x50 high-powered friend he could clearly see Box 48. It was fortunate that the parking lot serviced several other businesses so he was not conspicuous being 100 yards away.

LaFleur knew that after the terrorist attack on New York City of 9/11/01 the Postal Department required a picture ID and two types of evidence of physical address in order to rent a postal box but because this box had been opened over twenty years ago they did not require individuals to provide more proof than that which was used to rent the box originally. This meant that even a subpoena would get the name Vicki Chimes and a fake address. He decided that following her home was his only hope of finding her, of getting revenge. He'd show her.

~ 87 ~

For seemingly the umpteenth time the Criminal Investigation Division met in Gray. *Being a Detective in real life,* thought Reed, *is so different than what is depicted on television. "I'd like nothing better today than be involved in a high speed chase, followed by a "Go ahead, Punk, make my day," and concluding with a "Book 'em Dano."* Instead meetings, phone calls, interviews and waiting for lab results were the order of this, and virtually every, day.

Today's meeting was designed to allow fellow detectives to share information because, although many were working on the same case, they were following different leads and discovering new facts which could be important when combined with others. All of the regulars were there, most already seated as Reed raised his voice to get their attention.

"Gentlemen," he began, "It's time for a debriefing so that we can catch you up to speed and on the same page. I'll begin by sharing what Jake and I have learned about the woman who was allegedly raped twenty-plus years ago."

For the next twenty minutes Reed detailed their significant findings and the detectives were enthralled to hear about the birth of twins and how that shed a different light on the case. He also had Jake go over the info provided by Jackson Kelly including the fact that Tim Stockwell had been the primary on the alleged rape case.

Joe Quinn, as he often did, spoke first. "That explains who killed Andy LaFleur and why there was a common blood type with the first murderer, but it doesn't tell us who or where he is."

"Or what the correlation is to the woman," offered Bruce Costello. "Are these twins killing at the behest of the supposed mother or on their own? Have they been competing with one another or are they working in unison?"

"I'd like to try answering that Reed, if you don't mind" said

Walt Wizkowski. "I've got a couple of theories I'd like to offer."

"Go right ahead, Wiz" responded Reed. "What have you got?"

"Well, the introduction of a twin makes perfect sense to me because I believe the murders have been committed by two different people. If you look at the MO's and the notes left at the scene you can see the difference."

"The first girl killed, Angela Carrington, was in an apartment and a note was left on the wall painted in *her* blood. This is the same MO as the killing of Deanna Porter, the third girl murdered. The message was left there *in the dead girl's blood.*"

"Now lets examine the murders of Carrie Mortenson and Randy Kingston. In both of these murders it took place on a college campus outside, and in both instances a note was left at the scene but not painted and NOT in the blood of that person being killed. While the experts have determined that the handwriting was the same it was a note on paper in the previous victim's blood. Thus, the first murderer, the one called The Painter, may have written the notes at his home in the blood of the previous girl and then given the notes to his twin brother to leave at the scenes of his murders. Neither killer left prints, fibers, or other physical evidence except blood which turned out to not only be extremely rare but identical in DNA makeup."

"What about Andy LaFleur?" asked Frank Durgin.

"It follows the pattern," replied Wizkowski. "It appears that they took turns committing the murders and it was The Painter's turn. The fact that there was a small piece of paper with a message and a brush rather than the same size and style of note implies that perhaps he was going to paint a note inside the car or on its exterior. We know that when LaFleur actually does get killed there was a note left, a note in a different handwriting."

"Some good points Wiz," acknowledged Reed. "Although, as Guy suggested, in this case we don't really know the role of the woman, the mother, if any. Could these sons be doing these things on their own in some form of Oedipal repression or displacement?"

"What are some of the other things that you have been working on?" Reed asked the room in general.

"As you suggested," Wiz replied, "we have put a tail on Wallace LaFleur. He has been acting strangely of late - ever since you heard him allude to a woman being a 'fucking bitch' and stating defiantly that 'It didn't have to happen!'"

"We also have a man tailing Brandon Hancock just to make sure we haven't missed anything there," said Joe Lombardo. "I don't think it's him but we can't be too sure."

"And I'm still on the lookout for Tim Stockwell," added Jake. "I'm convinced there is something fishy there, what with him disappearing and all."

"Remember," said Reed. "According to earlier notes there are two more individuals slated to die. So not only are we trying to catch a killer but we are also trying to keep another pair alive - whomever and wherever they are."

~ 88 ~

Tim Stockwell took several more steps back and forth, looked out of the screened porch and took a deep swig off his Budweiser before asking Mike Pioretti for the tenth time, "What are we gonna do about this?"

"I don't know, Tim, but we'll come up with something," Pioretti replied. "That's why we came here - to think."

The two men had been ensconced at Pioretti's fishing camp on Upper Range Pond in Poland for three days. They had gone fishing once and discussed continually what should be their course of action after each had received a threatening letter. They had drank almost non-stop since they had arrived.

"I just don't get it, Mike, what on earth does she want?"

"You got me, Tim. I'm sure she just wants to scare us ...maybe get the last laugh"

"After all these years... why now? What does she want to prove, the cop asked rhetorically"

"Why do you keep asking me questions that I can't answer?" replied Mike as he polished off a Rolling Rock.

There on the porch coffee table sat a pair of letters addressed to the two men with identical messages inside:

YOU KNOW WHAT YOU DID WAS WRONG. IT IS TIME YOU MADE IT RIGHT!

MONEY CANNOT REPLACE YOUTH, INNOCENCE, OR A PERSON'S LIFE.

TO MAKE AMENDS PLAN ON VISITING NEXT FRIDAY. I WILL CALL WITH DIRECTIONS AND TIME.

YOU KNOW WHO!

"Where does she want us to go? What are we supposed to do?" Tim continued to ask questions although he did not expect answers from his companion. Grabbing another Budweiser from a cooler on the porch he tried to make sense of what both men dreaded.

"It was a long fucking time ago, Mike, we were young, foolish. We had futures, plans, places to go. Surely she can't hold that against us can she? You were on the fast track. Your future was assured as the DA. I had a chance to be Chief - shoulda' been. Christ O' Mighty those kids didn't mean nothing by that. They were just having a little fun – blowing off a little steam…that's all."

"I don't disagree with anything you're saying, Tim, but we both know that those Bowdoin kids went too far. It's one thing to watch her dance or even feel her up a little but raping her and using a beer bottle. That's not right."

"You're absolutely right and every one of them has now paid a terrible price - the death of a child. What more can she want? We didn't rape her."

"I guess we're just going to have to wait for her to call Friday and find out," said Mike finishing yet another Rolling Rock. "Hopefully we can come to some mutual agreement - but until that time I'm going to wait right here."

~ 89 ~

It was a good thing that Wallace LaFleur had come prepared because it was a much longer wait than he had expected. Although there was a hot dog vendor in the parking lot he did not want to be occupied when the time was right. For that reason he had packed sandwiches, drinks and even a couple of cookies - his own little picnic. He also had brought a large empty bottle in which to piss. He would take no chances. There was plenty of heat in his Lincoln Continental and he had WHOM 94.9 to keep him company. He hummed along to "I like pina coladas" by Rupert Holmes and waited. *Just like a typical broad,* he thought as he listened to the words of the song. *Never happy with what they have. They always want more.*

Because it was Friday, the end of the week, the post office seemed busier than normal. Despite the spike in activity, which kept Wallace LaFleur glued to his binoculars, the one person he wanted to see was nowhere to be found. It was almost 4:00 p.m. when he finally saw an individual place a key in Post Office Box 48. He was a bit confused because it was not a middle aged woman like he expected but rather a young man. Sure enough, he reached in, removed the large manila envelope that had been folded in half and removed it from the box. He placed it in the pocket of his gray wool coat and headed out of the Post Office.

LaFleur watched as the man walked to a tired looking red Dodge pickup and climbed in. After looking both ways he pulled forward and merged into the 302 traffic taking a right onto Route 35. He drove slowly, cautiously, perhaps in reverence to the condition of the truck. Unbeknownst to him a Lincoln Continental followed several hundred feet behind him.

LaFleur rubbed the outside of his leather bombardier jacket tracing the pistol he had brought for just this occasion. It had been in his possession for years, since back when he shot rats at the dump to impress his dates. *Ironic,* he thought. *I'm still shooting rats.*

The fact that there was someone else in the picture didn't phase LaFleur in the least. *In fact, if it was the bitch's son it would be even better, Yea, that would be poetic justice.*

He didn't fear being caught. He was much too shrewd to just go into their home and blast away. Besides, no one knew about the blackmailing. There would be no way to tie him to the murders. There would be no motive. Plus, who knows what her real name is. Thankfully, she had managed to keep that a secret all of these years.

He followed the truck for several miles along 35 until they came to the town of Sebago where he turned right onto 114. LaFleur thought how easy it was in Maine to follow someone, unlike any major city where the number of cars would have made it difficult to stay close. This was perfect as he had two vehicles between him and the red pickup – close enough to see where he was headed - far enough back to be inconspicuous.

After traveling 4-5 miles the truck slowed down, signaled and took a left onto what appeared to be a long winding driveway. The two cars who had been following the truck continued on and LaFleur did the same so as to not alert the person he was following. He went a short while further and pulled over into a vacant logging road. It would be dark shortly, he realized, and then he would go back down that winding driveway. There was no reason to be in a rush. He was much too shrewd, too calculating for that he rationalized. As always, he was in control. He would soon extract his revenge.

~ 90 ~

Tim Stockwell was almost glad that this would be over soon. Almost. He wasn't sure where, or into what, he was headed but after being away from his wife and job for almost five days he decided that closure with his mysterious host would be preferential to wondering. He didn't want this thing hanging over his head and he was tired of waiting.

He was also tired of wearing the same clothes. He didn't want to alarm his wife and he wasn't sure how long he'd be gone after receiving his letter so he hadn't packed a suitcase. Mike had a few items at the camp including a sweatshirt and jacket but Mike's pants didn't fit him and his own underwear were becoming downright rank. Thankfully it would soon be over.

He and Mike were en route to her home following the directions given over the phone. They had been instructed to take Pioretti's car and while Tim was a bit insecure without his cruiser, he had his weapon and would be on his highest alert.

After traveling for a little more than a half hour, coming in on the back side of what the locals called Big Sebago Lake, they were almost at their destination. With few homes and fewer landmarks in this sleepy little town it was not easy finding the unmarked driveway, especially as darkness was setting in, but at last they had found it.

As they turned into the driveway they saw a late model Lincoln Continental parked on the side of the road but thought nothing of it. The driveway was comprised of two thin trails of dirt where the tires had worn down any growth. Grass grew begrudgingly on a slight ridge in the middle. They followed the road for several hundred yards and made a pair of turns before an old white farmhouse and rundown barn came into view. The latter had support beams broken in the middle causing the structure to look like a tired camel. There was a pair of immense doors that slid across the outside to enclose whatever needed storing.

The road required a vehicle to go slowly or it would scrape the under carriage but they would have done so anyway. The only light they could see was in an upstairs window and it was neither bright nor inviting. Dark shutters hung from the windows in ill repair, broken and missing slats. As they arrived at the side of the house, where there was a bit of room to park, they could make out a clothesline, a large tract of land that probably was a garden in warmer weather, and a tree line surrounding the property in every direction. Tim saw the moon climbing above the majestic pines ahead and acknowledged the privacy this property provided.

"Since I don't see the welcome wagon hostess coming to greet us, I guess we'll have to go in."

"Kinda eerie isn't it?" replied Pioretti, slowly opening the driver's side door.

"Reminds me of the house behind the Bates Motel," admitted Stockwell, looking up to see if there were any faces or curtain movements. Seeing none he opened his door and tried to close it without making much noise.

As the two men walked slowly toward the porch they spied an open bulkhead just beyond with a faint fan of illumination being dispersed into the yard. Tim traced the weapon inside his jacket pocket and whispered to his partner, "Mike, let's take a look in the basement. Maybe we can learn something before we knock on the front door."

"Are you sure? That's going to look kinda funny if we're greeted down there. How are we going to explain our way out of that one?"

"Mike, I'm a police officer. You're a public official. We are simply looking out for the safety of the owner and guests. We don't want anyone to fall down this dimly lit stairway, now do we?"

"You lead the way, Tim. I'm behind you," said Pioretti, pulling up the collar on his coat.

~ 91 ~

Tim Stockwell advanced stealthily toward the open bulkhead, Mike Pioretti close behind. A lone light bulb covered in dust and hanging from a piece of wire provided a shard of light, enough to illuminate the cobwebs hanging from each corner thicker than pizza dough.

Four steps took them deeper into the basement where they were thrust into abstract darkness with the exception of another bulb hanging some distance ahead. They moved slowly, cautiously, toward the bulb. They were not sure where they were headed nor what they would find, but like moths they were drawn to the light.

Pioretti, a stride behind, whispered, "Why, if we were told to come here at a designated time, are we walking through the basement?"

Stockwell, instead of responding, put his right index finger to his lips and kept moving. On their right they came to stairs that seemed to lead up to the house and for a second Stockwell considered going up but then he looked at the long corridor that ran in front of them and decided against it. There would be time for that, he mused, and headed toward the lone, low-watt, bulb hanging ahead.

He wished he had brought a flashlight but rather than turn around he forged forward. On his left he was puzzled by what looked like a room carved out of rock with a dirt floor. He strained to see a stained mattress, small television resting on an orange crate, and a white plastic bucket in the corner. A small key hung on a nail outside the door. Opposite that room was another of equal size but with nothing inside of it. A few steps brought the Brunswick cop to another pair of rooms And then another. All were empty except one on the right that was furnished much like the earlier one. The dank stench of urine and feces was overbearing. The walkway ran under the farmhouse and beyond, damp and dark; also hewn out of dirt and stone.

"What do you make of this," Pioretti asked Stockwell.

"I can't imagine. It looks and smells like someone has been living in these rooms."

"Should we go upstairs? I can't imagine that whoever is in this house doesn't know we're down here."

"If so, then why haven't they come down to greet us?" asked Stockwell

"Maybe they wanted us to see this - or something else. Should we keep going?"

"We've come this far. The end can't be much further."

Once again the two men continued forward now walking away from the lone bulb that illuminated the cramped walkway bending slightly to avoid hitting their heads. Walking beside one another, they turned a corner before it straightened out and despite the darkness, a couple of dozen feet in front of them, they saw a large shape filling almost the entire area from the dirt floor to the wooden crossbeam stretched across the ceiling.

From their distance they couldn't discern what it was but after taking several silent steps Stockwell saw there was another bulb hanging down further ahead with a pull string beside it. He reached, gave a slight pull and the area was cast in shrouded light - enough to let the two men see that the shape hanging in front of them, with a hook through his bombardier jacket, and his throat cut from ear to ear - was Wallace LaFleur. His eyes were glazed and open seeming to stare in horror at the ceiling. Stockwell stepped closer, looked at the dead man's open mouth and saw that between his lips, into his throat, had been wedged a bloody shaft of flesh. Looking down LaFleur's body he confirmed his suspicions - it was his penis.

Stockwell fell to his knees and vomited on the dirt floor.

The feminine voice behind them said, "Welcome."

~ 92 ~

Stockwell tried to reach for his revolver but on his hands and knees he was in a compromising position and the voice behind him knew that as well.

"Now don't do anything stupid. Reach slowly in and remove your gun.Stockwell did as he was told while Pioretti, frozen with both revulsion and fear, held his ground without moving a muscle. He realized that he was holding his breath and was forced to make a deep exhalation.

"Throw your gun behind you. Now lift your right pant leg and remove the knife you have strapped there," said the woman in a calm yet authoritative voice. "Put that behind you, as well."

"*How in the hell did she know that,* thought Stockwell. *There are guys on the force with me that don't know I carry 'Ole Betsy' …and where have I heard that voice?*"

Pioretti's face showed a comparable degree of bewilderment but he said nothing.

The woman bent to pick up the two weapons and as that was being done she once again spoke. "I see that you have found my latest guest, the powerful Wallace LaFleur. He doesn't look quite so formidable today does he? He's not quite so domineering, so defiant, so high and mighty with his cock in his mouth. I'm sure he came here thinking he would extract revenge for the death of his son but ironically it seems that it is I who have enjoyed revenge - revenge that has been a long time in the planning. Stroking his dick so that it got nice and hard and then cutting it off while he was still alive was one of my life's greatest pleasures.

Both men found themselves looking up at LaFleur's face and intrinsically shuddering at what must have been a horrific experience. Stockwell asked the question that he had ruminated on for several days,

"What do you want from us?"

"Why, what anyone would want - justice. Certainly you two

217

men can understand that, having spent your lives providing justice to the communities that you represent. Aren't you sworn to uphold the laws and protect those that you serve?"

Stockwell paused for a moment as he listened trying to place the deep voice in the tunnel but before he could respond his partner spoke up, "Yes we are and we do," stuttered Pioretti. "But we're human - we can make mistakes. Look, miss, I am so very sorry for what occurred to you. I was wrong. We were wrong. But it was such a long time ago. Surely you can understand that?"

"All I understand, Mr. District Attorney," she spat at him, "is that you had no trouble taking Wallace LaFleur's money to not bring my case to trial. How much did he pay you, $50,000… $100,000, a guarantee that you would become the DA?"

"I was young then," he almost whined. "The money seemed like a fortune and becoming the DA was my dream."

"Fuck you, Pioretti. I had dreams too. Instead I got nightmares. Years of nights waking up in a sweat, screaming, crying, with men clawing at my body, ramming beer bottles inside me."

"I said I was sorry," he began again. "What can I do to make it up to you?"

"Very simple counselor, you may walk straight ahead until you reach Mr LaFleur. I want to be fair and it seems only fair that you join Wally in everlasting darkness."

With no warning a strong, young man, dressed only in underwear and clenching a seven inch hunting knife in his right hand came up behind Pioretti and grabbed him under the arm. The DA attempted to struggle but the younger man's brute strength and element of surprise gave him no option but to comply. Stockwell watched as his friend and partner in evil was literally dragged down the dark dirt corridor.

Stockwell, still on his knees, began to slowly turn around - away from the oncoming carnage, but her voice resonated. "Don't you turn around. You keep looking so you can see the true meaning of the word justice. He should be thankful that, since he had no role in the rape itself, his genitalia will remain intact."

Stockwell once again recoiled in horror as he watched the nearly naked man behind Pioretti, hold him tight in a headlock and then casually run the serrated edge of the hunting knife along his lower neck. Pioretti flailed in an attempt to escape but it was too late. Blood spurted from his throat while his arms wind-milled against his assailant. His legs shook spastically trying alternately to both get away and kick the man that was holding him. After several seconds his eyes bulged from his head and a last gurgle escaped from his throat before he made one last twitch and his head fell sideways against his shoulder. After holding him a short while longer the naked man let him slide to the ground in a sitting position, his upper torso resting against LaFleur in death's last dance.

Stockwell fell forward onto his hands and again attempted to vomit but this time it was more dry heaves and bile that escaped his lips, his stomach wracked with searing spasms. He opened his eyes, his mind racing as to his next move.

The woman in control, with his revolver pointed at him said, "Now Mr. Stockwell it's time we got to know each other a little bit better."

"I know who you are, you murdering bitch, You are Vicki Chimes."

"Oh really, she replied. Then why don't you slowly turn around."

Stockwell did as he was told and turned very slowly on his knees assuming that his weapon was being pointed at him. He did not, however, expect to see who was standing in front of him. OHHH MY GOD, he wailed as he looked up at the woman standing in front of him wearing a tattered D2MAD t-shirt. ZULMA! NO, IT CAN'T BE YOU! ...NOT MY DAUGHTER!"

~ 93 ~

"Don't you dare call me your daughter you sonofabitch! I stopped being your daughter when I walked out of the house. I stopped being your daughter when you made me do those things with you. 'Mom has gone to visit Aunt Ruth this weekend why don't we play house like Daddy and Mommy do,' her voice spat in bitter imitation. "For years you had me play house or play 'Mommy' and I didn't know any better." Her voice was rising. 'It will be our little secret,' you said. 'We don't need to tell Mommy because then her feelings will be hurt. She will feel like someone is trying to take her place. This is OUR game,' "you said, you miserable bastard. And then, even after Mom would come home, you would wake me up late at night. After she was asleep you would come into my room and get into my bed and you would climb on top of me. You hurt me so badly but you said it would go away, that it would soon feel good and that when I was older that I would thank you for all that you had taught me." Her voice now was starting to crack and tears were running down her cheeks "Then you would come home from work after I got home from school and Mom was still working and you would take down your pants and make me do things. For weeks, months, years this went on and I never said a word. I never understood that this was not right. I wanted to make you happy. I wanted to be a good girl like you said."

Tim Stockwell stood there with a gun pointed at him and listened as twenty plus years of pent up rage was spewed like machine gun bullets at the man she once called "Daddy."

He had no idea what to say he just knew that he had to try and get out of this predicament. He had seen how little remorse she showed Mike Piorotti and this was the same woman who had masterminded at least six other murders. He had to keep her talking.

"When did you become Vicki Chimes?"

"After I moved out of our happy home," she said sarcastically. "I moved in with a guy who was stationed at the base. I got some jobs and finally earned my GED. I was doing great and planned to go to college that fall. In order to save enough money I started working for Passionate Pleasures as a dancer and found out that I could take home $500 a week. And then it happened. The night that changed my life, what there was of it, forever. Five selfish, arrogant Bowdoin pukes who thought they could get away with anything. Well, you know what? They could, and they did - thanks to a scumbag lawyer and a dirty cop on the take." She was walking in a small area in front of him, her voice again rising, the weapon being waved menacingly.

"Christ! I had no idea that you were Vicki Chimes. I just knew that I would get a fat chunk of change from Wally LaFleur if I could make the whole thing go away. I never interviewed you, I just falsified the report making it look like I did. I never even saw you for God sakes. How was I to know that you were Vicki Chimes?"

"You weren't, don't you see? You cared so little about the victim, about *the person* that even though you were designated as the primary detective on the case you never even interviewed the girl involved. I told the truth to some cop named Kelly and you buried it. I was assaulted, raped, sodomized, and brutalized and not one person spent one day in jail for the crime! So I decided there and then that if the system wouldn't work for me, then I would change the system. Revenge, frontier justice, kadachiuchi, it's all the same. If you can't trust those who are being paid to protect you then you need to take matters into your own hands."

"If only I had known that you were behind this…"

"Then what?…you had already spent years molesting me, raping me. How the fuck is it any different?" You spent all that time borrowing against my future and today the loan comes due. It's time to pay the fiddler, … "Daddy."

"Now, you take off *your* clothes."

~ 94 ~

Reed got the call shortly before dark. Walt Wizkowski had been trailing Wallace LaFleur for several days and when he saw him stakeout, and then follow, a pickup from the Windham Post Office to a desolate driveway in Sebago he was convinced that this was the "real deal." He also watched as Tim Stockwell and the District Attorney, Mike Pioretti went inside. None of the three had resurfaced.

Wiz immediately contacted Reed, who got in touch with Jake, and several other detectives as well as Special Reaction Teams from both the MSP and the Cumberland County Sheriff's Department. Reed and Jake arrived at the site long before the others and those two plus Wizkowski discussed their options from their position in the driveway.

While Reed knew the proper protocol was to wait for the specially trained officers to take precedence under their Commander, he also knew that there were at least three individuals inside who might be in grave danger. He made a decision. "Jake, I'm going in. Every minute counts and I don't want to wait for the cavalry. Are you with me?"

"I'm good to go, partner. Lead the way."

"Wiz, you stay here in case someone looks to leave the building and send in the others when they arrive."

The two men walked partway up the driveway together before splitting up and circum-navigating the house. They were at opposite ends of the building when they saw the open bulkhead and misty light. A thick, damp fog had settled in over much of the landscape and the moisture in the air was heavy enough to restrict vision from a few feet.

Reed signaled Jake to follow him and they headed for the entrance to the cellar. At the bottom they were attracted by another light and a far off voice. They walked slowly toward both pausing to listen after every couple of steps. Reed could hear, but not identify, either the raised feminine voice or the recipient of her rant.

Passing in front of the steps leading upstairs the men split again so they were on opposite sides of the dark, dirt corridor. Neither could yet see the origin of the diatribe but the tone was unmistakable - someone was being rebuked and Reed assumed that the speaker was the target of their entry; the mystery woman they had been searching for.

Both men observed the "room" on the left and rolled their eyes at the visualization of what must have been. Because of the bends in the corridor they could not be seen advancing but conversely, neither could they yet see what they wanted. Both had their weapons drawn as they ever-so-slowly inched toward the bend.

Reed leaned his body against the wall so that just his head was given clearance around the corner. He could now see a woman, back-to, with a revolver in her hand and in front of her, totally nude, was Tim Stockwell, whose arms were now tied behind his head, with what looked like clothesline rope. He was being led into a room on Reed's left by a nearly nude man in underwear with blood splattered all over his body.

Both detectives could now hear the woman who was raising her voice in an emotional state; "REMEMBER DADDY, HOW YOU ALWAYS SAID YOU WERE THE MAN OF THE HOUSE. HOW I WAS TO OBEY YOU BECAUSE YOU WERE THE HEAD OF THE FAMILY. HOW YOU WOULD ALWAYS TAKE THE BEST CHAIR AT THE HEAD OF THE TABLE. YOU WERE THE KING OF THE CASTLE AND DESERVED A THRONE, YOU SAID... THEN YOU WOULD HAVE ME SIT IN YOUR LAP WITH A TABLECLOTH COVERING ME SO YOU COULD RUB BETWEEN MY LEGS WITHOUT ANY ONE SEEING. I HAVE HAD A LOT OF TIME TO REMEMBER... AND THINK... AND PLAN FOR THIS DAY, DADDY, AND LIKE YOU SAID, YOU ARE THE KING AND DESERVE A THRONE. SO I BUILT YOU ONE, ESPECIALLY FOR YOU. LOOK DADDY ISN'T IT SPECIAL!"

Tears were running down her cheeks and her voice was cracking with the pent-up pain of life's lost years.

As the woman turned and stood facing into the entrance of a

room on the left Reed recognized that the woman had what looked like a 45 Glock, a police weapon of choice, probably Stockwell's. He contemplated his options. He assumed the near-naked man was also armed and if they were detected they would be open and vulnerable in the middle of a corridor. They needed to wait until either the woman went totally inside the room with Stockwell or until they came down the corridor where they could be ambushed as they came around the corner. The problem with the latter option, Reed thought, was that it might be too late to save Stockwell and anyone else being held captive inside.

Stockwell looked with frozen fear at the specially designed wooden chair built to look like a throne with wide armrests, a tall back and protruding up the center a twelve inch spiral metal rod that was a half-inch wide at the base and rose to a sharp point. He tried to lurch quickly in an attempt to escape but the young man, who held him by the rope above his head, was prepared for his attempt and literally threw him toward the chair. As the man dragged him from behind Stockwell lost his balance and just before he was forced onto the chair his blood-curdling screams reverberated through the tunnel.

"ZULMA, ZULMA, NO!!! ...DON'T MAKE ME SIT ON THAT, PLEASE!...PLEASE!...HAVE MERCY!...AAAHHHH!"

A wry smile broke across her face. "MERCY, MY ASS! MAY YOU ROT IN HELL YOU BASTARD... JUSTICE IS FINALLY SERVED. FUCK YOU... 'DADDY.'"

As she offered her final denigration to her biological father she watched him take his last breaths engulfed with pain, his eyes rolling back into his head.

The screaming stopped when once again the young man behind him raked his knife across the neck of the Brunswick cop.

Reed and Jake had moved slowly, stealthily when the screams had begun. They were almost up to the room when they saw Wallace LaFleur hanging above Mike Pioretti; both men with their throats cut, a pool of blood staining the dirt floor. Revulsion gripped both men but they kept moving. As they drew almost even with the opening Reed's foot came into contact with a loose rock on the side of the wall dislodging it and sending it rolling along the basement floor. Suddenly, the man dressed only in a pair of underwear, charged out of the room, directly at him, a hunting knife raised above his head.

Before he had time to move his arm downward Jake fired two rounds from his H&K into the man's chest, sending his knife flying, knocking him backward onto the floor. Blood seeped from the corner of his mouth, but refusing to stay down, he grabbed the loose rock and leaned toward Reed who had stepped back to avoid the attack. He brought the rock against Reed's knee before another bullet from Jake's revolver entered his skull behind his ear sending brain matter into the wall and his body onto Reed's feet.

The woman, whom Reed heard called "Zulma" by Stockwell, stepped deeper into the darkness behind her father's "throne" rather than come out of the room. Reed and Jake were now on either side of the small chamber, the dead body of Tim Stockwell between them. Both detectives had their weapons drawn.

Reed spoke first, "I heard you called Zulma and I know that not only are you Stockwell's daughter but that you have gone by the name Vicki Chimes. What would you like me to call you, miss?"

"Call me Vicki, I stopped being 'Zulma' a long time ago."

"Alright, Vicki it is. My name is Reed Sanderson and this is my partner Jake Lewis. We are detectives with the Maine State Police. I need you to put the gun down and come out of there with your hands up, Vicki. You're going to have to come with us."

"Why, so I can pay a penalty for getting rid of those low-lives? I ought to get a medal for doing your work - for finally providing justice where there has been none. All those years of being molested by my own father ... and then being raped and assaulted by those Bowdoin students only to have it just brushed under the carpet... having Wally LaFleur pay off both my father and Pioretti to have it go away. No, I don't think I want to leave it up to the so-called legal system again."

"Vicki, listen," Reed began. "I know how hard it must have been for you ..."

"Oh no you don't. Don't pretend to know about something that you have no knowledge of. How could you? Have you been raped, sodomized, brutalized? Have you been sexually abused by the man who gave you life, who was supposed to love you, teach you, protect you?"

"No, I haven't, but I promise you that you'll get a fair trial. All that will be taken into consideration."

"Well, Detective Sanderson, I have already taken all of this into consideration. I have spent the last few weeks getting even, *getting justice* and now, as then, I must do the right thing to balance the scales. I am not sorry for anything my boys or I have done. In my mind it was the right thing to do but now there is only one way that this can truly end fairly." She raised the gun to her head.

"Vicki, NO!" Reed shouted. "Don't you see. There has been enough pain, enough blood shed. There is nothing to be gained by killing yourself."

But it was too late. She never heard Reed's last plea as the bullet ripped through her skull bringing darkness to a life that had already been cursed with so much of the same.

Reed now noticed the throbbing pain in his knee as he turned and faced his partner who was on the opposite side of the entrance, his gun still drawn. Reed walked over, past the body of Tim Stockwell, looked down at the lifeless woman and said quietly, "C'mon, Jake, let's get the hell out of here."

Rushing down the basement corridor were several troopers led by Joe Lombardo.

"Holy jumped-up Jesus Christ," he said, looking at the carnage of bodies hung, laying with their throats cut. "What the hell went on down here?"

"All that matters Guy," said Reed heading for the exit, "is that it's finally over. I'll turn in my report in the morning."

"I'll take care of that, said Jake. You go on home. Obviously there will be a lot of follow-up investigation and paperwork, but in the meantime, you need to go home and take care of yourself. If I'm not mistaken you've got a fishing trip to plan."

~ 95 ~

Scott was busy stirring the frosting for the birthday cake that Sandy was baking.

"You know, Scotty boy, you keep eating that frosting and there isn't going to be enough for the cake."

"Sampling… Sandy, not eating. Everyone knows that great chefs sample their gourmet offerings."

"Since when does carrot cake with cream cheese frosting constitute gourmet cooking?" asked Sandy, as he stuck a piece of broom in the confection checking to see if it was done.

"When it's Dad's birthday," responded Scott.

"You've got a point there, I guess, which means that cheeseburgers and French Fries fall into that category on your birthday, right Scotty?"

"Of course not …but Bacon cheeseburgers and curly fries, that's different."

Reed walked into the kitchen and glanced around at the plates, measuring cups, pans, bowls and ingredients spread out around the table and counter tops and said, "Are we having a yard sale or is there some actual cooking going on here?"

"You'll eat those words, shortly my extinguished friend," said Sandy

"Don't you mean distinguished?" Reed asked.

"No, extinguished. 'Cause I'm putting you out of here," Sandy replied playfully, pushing his son into the living room.

"What's the main course?" Reed asked, before sitting on the sofa.

"We're not sure, Dad, Mom said she would take care of that. She should be here any minute."

"Probably a nice spinach quiche with cous cous and some chick peas," suggested Sandy.

"That'll be alright," shouted Reed from the living room. "Barney's got to have something to eat."

At that point Amy walked in with a casserole bowl covered with foil. Hey everyone, can I get a hand bringing in the things in the back seat?"

"I'll do it Mom."

Reed walked into the room straight to Amy's arms. "Hi Darling."

"Happy Birthday, Reed," she replied with a kiss. "Hungry?"

"Hungry enough to eat the north end of a south bound skunk."

"Could you come up with a little classier response?" she replied.

"I was taught to let your words paint pictures," laughed Reed.

The four sat down to a meal of baked stuffed shrimp, mashed potatoes and Caesar salad complete with anchovies, Reed's favorite meal.

"How was it?" she asked as she rose to help clear the table.

"Not bad, if you like perfect," Reed replied.

"I'm glad you liked it. You deserved it after all you've been through lately. The last time we had one of these family dinners we were fooled. Is this really the end of those senseless killings?"

"It's finally over," Reed acknowledged. "Until the next time, the next crime."

"Time for desert Dad," said Scott, "and then presents."

Reed watched as Scott brought out the carrot birthday cake complete with 44 candles distributed around the top.

"You realize of course that I had to get a burning permit in order to light this," said Sandy bending over to light each candle individually. "It would be easier with a flame-thrower."

After everyone had a piece of cake and complimented the frosting chef on his work, Scott walked into his bedroom and came back with a wrapped present which prompted Sandy to do the same. Inside the two packages were a hand drawn map to their camp on Moose Lake, a fishing lure and a book entitled "Pictorial History of the Big Fish Caught by Reed Sanderson" When Reed opened it he found a complete journal of blank white pages.

"Very funny, you two," he said. "A not-so-subtle hint as to where we're headed tomorrow I guess."

"Well," Amy said, "then I had better clean up so I can go home and pack."Reed looked at her with a air of amazement, "You're coming to the fishing camp with us?" he asked.

"Mom," Scott interrupted, "Give Dad your present."

"Well I don't know how much of a present it is … but, if you'll have me, I'd like to move back in with you guys." Tears welled in Reed's eyes as what Amy had just said sunk in. "Oh Darling. Are you sure?"

"I'm very sure. I've come to the realization that everything in life is filled with risks and I can't run away from that. If we are going to face life's challenges I want to do it together - as a family."

"No offense guys, but this may be my best birthday present ever," said Reed as he wrapped his arms around Amy.

"Before you get all ga ga I figure that we should vote," said Sandy … "it could be close …"

"God Bless you Dad, you never let up, do you?"

EPILOGUE

Joseph "Snake" Mercier rode his Harley Davidson Night Train down Route 93 south towards his destination in Quincy Massachusetts. He had paid almost $13,000 for this 2003 Vivid Black model but he had needed some form of transportation since he had lost the use of the Cadillac Escalade he and his brother had purchased last year.

He lamented the loss of that flashy SUV but far more he felt the pain of losing his brother in a shoot-out with the Maine State Police. Since that day he had moved in with a group belonging to the East Coast White Unity in Quincy and not a day went by that his mind did not take him back to that day and the day three years earlier when his father died following a scuffle with Jake Lewis.

He had felt bad at first when he had learned that his brother had inadvertently killed a kid. They had planned to snuff Jake on that drive by. How the hell was he to know that some cop's kid would be driving Jake's car. Now, after having his only brother taken out by Jake and his buddy Reed Sanderson, he was glad that they had offed the little bastard. But that was not going to be the end of his retaliation – not by a long shot.

He laughed at the pun he had made in his head. *Not by a long shot.* No. He wanted to make it a close shot or better yet, shots. He wanted to not only see those two mother fuckers die, he wanted to see them suffer. *It's only fitting,* he thought. *They're such good buddies and go so many places with each other that it's only fair that I send them to hell together.*